PATTAYA PSYCHO

EDWARD SWEENEY

(1) WELCOME TO THE LENNY PAZAZZ SHOW

(2) THE RETURN OF THE OTHER CLOWNS

(3) PATTAYA DOES NOT APPEAL TO EVERYONE

(4) JACK AND KENNY FACE DANGER

(5) AND THEN THERE WERE SIX

(6)   SO THAT'S HIM, IS IT?

(7)   A STRANGE FRIENDSHIP

(8)   GIRLS LIKE A BIT OF FUN, TOO

(9)   WITH FRIENDS LIKE THESE…

(10)   BLACKMAIL

(11)   THERE'S NOTHING I LIKE BETTER THAN A GOOD MURDER

(12)   WE ARE ALL GONNA MISS THIS PLACE

NOTE

This book is a work of fiction. Any similarity to persons living or dead is entirely coincidental.

CHAPTER ONE

WELCOME TO THE LENNY PAZAZZ SHOW

Pattaya, Thailand. A crowded bar in Soi 13. Lenny Pazazz and his sidekick Seamus O'Connor are hosting a live Youtube show from Lenny's bar.

'Hello, good evening and welcome to the show. This is Lenny Pazazz here bringing you what's new in the fun filled entertainment capital of the world, Pattaya'.

'And I'm Seamus O'Connor and in between having to put up with Lenny and his annoying chatter I'll be giving you the latest, up to date information that you need before you visit the party capital of the world'.

Lenny: 'Am I really that annoying, Seamus? I'm sure you don't really mean that.'

Seamus, nodding to the camera. 'Yes, I do.'

Lenny, a little wounded but keeping the same, cheesy, Seventies DJ smile: 'Well, as we head toward high season in the Land Of Smiles we'll be answering your questions, giving a few helpful hints and showing you what lovely ladies we have in the bar here tonight. Remember, all you have to do is smash that like button, subscribe to our YouTube channel if you haven't already and any Superchats will go towards buying the girls a drink. Please give generously. You know you wanna!'

NING: A VERY THAI GIRL

In a cozy hotel room in Pattaya, Ning was lying on her back getting shagged by an ageing farang.

Ning: 'Oh, sweetheart, you are the best, you are the best.'

Colin: 'Ohhh, arrrhhhhhh.....am I?   Arrrhhhhhhh......ooooooohhhhhh....'

Ning: 'Arrrrhhh, honey, I miss you when you go home. I cry when you leave.'

Colin, trying to stay hard: 'I'll be back, baby. Arrrrrhhhh, you'd better believe it.'

Ning continued to lay back as this obese, sweaty English farang pounded her with his withered, sixty year old cock. So enjoying the moment Colin was that he didn't notice that Ning was holding up her smartphone checking the texts she was receiving from various other farangs.

When the ordeal was over, Ning was escorted by Colin, a fat Englishman whose three week holiday was now at an end, downstairs to reception where she was to collect her identity card.

Pie was the receptionist. She knew Ning from old, had seen her at this hotel many times with many farangs. Pie, who was almost fifty, wondered how much money Ning could make at her game. She must be worth a fortune by now, Pie thought. As she approached reception holding hands with another gullible farang, Pie could tell by Ning's smile that she had ensnared another sponsor. Pie was lucky if she got a tip from these old bastards.

Ning collected her identity card from Pie and was led outside to a waiting taxi. Often she would get an inflated taxi fare from her customer and then get a cheaper motorbike taxi and pocket the difference. This time, with moneybags Colin, she decided to treat herself to a Bolt cab.

Colin, holding Ning tight on the steps of the hotel: 'I'm gonna miss you, Ning. You've been the best thing that's happened to me in years.'

Ning, smiling as she looked into the hideous fat face of Colin: 'I'm going to think of you everyday, Colin. You have a safe flight home, my sweetheart.'

Colin kissed her a long, passionate kiss. How romantic, Ning thought. Just so long as the fat old bastard has her bank account number so he could send her that money every month, she'd play along with any game.

Colin waved to Ning as she got into the taxi. He stood on the steps looking sad to be leaving. He had had a wonderful holiday in Pattaya and Ning was the beautiful girl of his dreams. He was so lucky to have met her. Ning waved back until she was out of sight of the hotel. Then she pulled out her smartphone and checked her texts once again. More messages of love from gullible farangs. There was Frankie, from England, Tomas, the German, and Marco, the Italian, and a voicemail from Lee, another English farang. This one was in the last half hour. Ning pressed the voice mail.

'Surprise surprise! How are you Ning, my Darling? It's Lee here and guess what! I'm in town. I arrived in Pattaya this morning. Let's meet up this afternoon. Can't wait to see you again. I've soooooo missed you, my honey.'

Ning put her phone back into her handbag, and stared out the window as the taxi sped through the streets of Pattaya. She thought for a while, and eventually cried out: 'Ohhhhh, FUCK!'

JACK AND KENNY

The taxi pulled up in the narrow street in Pattaya. It was November and it was a scorcher of a day.

'Is this the right one?' one of the guys in the taxi said. The taxi driver turned around and said something like, 'Yes, Beverly hotel.'

'It looks different from the photos,' the other one said.

'It looks smaller but it's the right one. Let's get out.'

The two men got out of the taxi and paid the driver three thousand baht plus a hundred baht tip. Airport rates, but still pretty good for a one and a half hour journey from Bangkok Suvarnabhumi. Two porters rushed down the steps to collect their suitcases and open the doors wide for them to enter.

Kenny: 'Looks alright inside.'

Jack: 'I'd stay in a dog kennel as long as it's not with the other fucking clowns.'

The two men entered the hotel and went over to the reception area. Jack hated this bit. Getting your passport out, filling in the same laborious forms and all that crap. After a long journey from Liverpool, 30 hours if you add up all the coach journeys and flights via Dubai and the waiting and the checking in and then from Bangkok to Pattaya, he just wanted to get in that hotel room and crash out.

'Sawadeeka, gentlemen', the friendly, pudgy receptionist said with a cheesy Thai smile and a Wai. 'Your name, please.'

Jack and Kenny went through all the Laborious stuff with the friendly receptionist. They were then shown to their rooms by a porter who had the cheesiest grin of all. 'You're from Liverpool,' the young Thai man said in the lift. Jack and Kenny nodded. 'I love Liverpool,' the porter said. He then put his arms in the air as if waving a scarf. 'Liverpoooooolllll!!!'

Oh, Christ, Jack thought. Not being a football fan he could do without this. Kenny, however, laughed. He was a football fan and could talk for hours about football. And probably would now he had met this guy.

Jack and Kenny had separate double rooms next to each other on the seventh floor. The views over the town were pretty good. The beach view was the other side of the building. They were staying in Soi 7, close to the action. The rooms look alright. Not the Ritz, but comfortable, clean looking and not too expensive.

After dumping their luggage off at the hotel, Jack and Kenny took a short walk to a Beach Road bar at the end of Soi 7.

Jack, swigging his cold Singha: 'Ahhhh, this is the life. Makes me wonder why I took so long to catch onto Winter Sunshine.'

Kenny: 'Yeah, you're right, there. They're freezing their bollocks off back home. This is the place to be.'

Jack: 'I know I keep going on about this, but I'm so relieved we haven't got the other fucking losers with us. The last thing I need is for some prick to start tapping me for money.'

Kenny, nodded. This was their second visit to Thailand. The first time there were five of them. Jack, Kenny and three friends who hadn't a clue how to manage their spending money and caused all kinds of shit. Kenny understood where Jack was coming from, but he still had a feeling he was going to miss the 'other fucking clowns', as Jack liked to call them.

THE LENNY PAZAZZ SHOW

'And on the sexy couch tonight we have a bevy of beautiful hostesses who are just dying to meet you,' Lenny Pazzaz said, grinning at the camera.

Seamus rolled his eyes. 'Just be honest, Lenny. They're after your money.' Seamus grinned at the camera. 'Hey, you out there. Look at all these lovelies on the couch flashing their tits and asses. Now get your superchats coming in and buy them all a drink.'

Lenny Pazzaz grimaced at his colleague's abrasive humour, and wondered once again if he had made a wise decision having him as co-host on the show. Fact is, Seamus was a shareholder in Lenny's company so he was kind of stuck with him.

Lenny: 'Let's introduce the girls. Amree, zoom that camera in on these lovely ladies. And not too naughty, either, ladies. This is Youtube, not Pornhub, remember.'

Amree, the Thai cameraman, zoomed into the couchful of Thai girls flashing their cleavage. A couple of them pushed their tits out for the camera.

Seamus: 'And on the couch tonight we have the lovely Fon in the revealing blue dress.' Fon smiled for the camera and gave a friendly wave. 'Next up we have Aom.' Aom smiled, but didn't seem so enthusiastic. 'Next we have Malee'. Marlee was overweight but hopeful someone may like her enough to send her some money. 'Next it's the ever so sexy Fran.' Fran was a real hottie, a Milf or around thirty with a lovely body. 'And last but by no means least it's Doil.' Doi was a regular star who liked a drink and sometimes got visibly drunk on the show. Always good for a laugh.

Lenny: 'So, guys, that's our lovely lineup for the night. Remember, send a superchat and buy the hotties a drink. I'm sure they'll love you for it.'

WALKING STREET

Kenny: 'Fuck me, this place gets more and more expensive!'
Jack, smooching up with a topless go go dancer in a Walking Street club. 'Why is that?   Have you asked her how much?'

Kenny, also smooching with a topless bird: 'Yes. She wants five fucking thousand for long time and two thousand for a bar fine.'

Jack: 'As well as all those lady drinks you've bought her. That's fucking expensive. Just make damn sure you get a good hard on to justify that price.'

Kenny: 'I'm not doing it. Fuck me, that's about the best part of two hundred quid in total. Need to be a fucking millionaire to live it up in this place.'

Jack and Kenny had only been to Pattaya once before, but were wise to the prices by now. They also knew all that 'everything's dirt cheap in Thailand ' was a load of bollocks. That was the bullshit that you heard back home, usually from people who'd never been here.

The two guys paid for their bill and left the go go bar. It wasn't a good feeling leaving those topless beauties behind. Both Jack and Kenny would like to have brought them back to the hotel and had steamy sex with them, but, like Kenny said, you need to be mega flush with money to enjoy Pattaya to the full, and they were no millionaires.

They walked through Walking Street and, ignoring all the signs for drinks promotions, found a familiar little bar on one of the corner sois. They ordered a couple of beers and sat down. At least watching the world go by didn't cost much money.

Kenny: 'It looks like it's more expensive here now than last time we were here.'

Jack: 'Well, it is what it is. Once we get away from this Walking Street area it gets cheaper. Go go bars are not for cheap charlies.'

Kenny: 'I may get myself a nice, regular bit of stuff. Might work out cheaper. Isn't that what you did last time?'

Jack: 'Yes, I had a regular. Minnie her name was. She was great. But, don't forget, they're all opportunistic and looking for a sponsor. And if you're with her all the time it means you will pay double the price wherever you go. Nothing's cheap here, regardless of what they tell you back home.'

'Scousers, eh? What part of the pool are you from, lads?'

Jack and Kenny swung around in their chairs to see a grinning English bloke with a Northern accent. He seemed friendly enough.

Kenny: 'Well, I'm from Huyton and he's from the North end somewhere.'

Jack: 'Are you on holiday here?'

The friendly guy sat at the table with them. 'Name's Lee. I'm paying a surprise visit to my girlfriend. Got a bit of time off work and I just thought, what the fuck, so I booked a flight out here. Last minute stuff. Cost me one and half grand. Flights are fucking expensive.'

Jack: 'Well, where is she now?'

Lee, shrugging: 'I don't know. She's stopped answering my calls and has disappeared all of a sudden. I've been to the bar where I met her and they say she hasn't worked there for months.'

Jack and Kenny looked knowingly at each other. Was this another gullible farang?

Jack: 'So you're here alone? Never mind, join us. Let's have another beer.'

Jack called the waitress over and ordered another round for the three. Lee seemed a decent enough guy so it would be nice to have company.

Kenny: 'So what are you gonna do, Lee? I mean, she might not be here. She might have gone home to her village. That's what some of these girls do, isn't it?'

Lee: 'I don't know. I just don't get it. I've been sending her money every month, she's been excited every time I send her a message or talk to her on skype. Now she's just disappeared. I'm a bit worried.'

Jack: 'How much have you been sending her each month?'

Lee, hesitant at first before answering that: 'I've been sending her forty thousand baht a month. But now she says that's not enough to live on. She wants sixty thousand a month. I just don't know what to do.'

Jack and Kenny looked blankly at each other again. Forty thousand baht was almost a grand in English money. And she said she wants one and a half times that.

Kenny: 'Lee, you seem like a good guy. But, come on, that's a lot of money out here. Are you sure she's not taking you for a mug?'

Lee grimaced at Kenny. He clearly didn't like that. 'What are you trying to say? I'm no mug. What are you trying to say?'

Kenny regretted his lack of subtlety. 'Lee, I don't mean offence. I'm only trying to help. Fact is, you've been sending her this money and now she's not even here to meet you. You've got to question that. I mean, why didn't you tell her you were coming out here?'

Lee, looking sad and pathetic: 'I thought I'd pay her a surprise visit. I mean, I love the girl. I've been out here three times and we've stayed together and she's even planning on coming to England to live with me.'

Jack, thinking he spotted something: 'Lee, when you've met her here before, did you let her know you were coming? Is this the first time you have paid her a surprise visit?'

Lee nodded: 'Yes. Spur of the moment thing. Now it's all gone dead. Can't get in touch with her. She's just not answering my calls.'

The three drank more beers together and had a quiet night watching the Pattaya world go by. Jack and Kenny were glad they had made a new friend. It took their minds off the other clowns, wherever they were now.

Lee, looking sad and foolish: 'I feel like a fool. I love the girl so much. Just couldn't wait to see her again. I just haven't got a clue where she is right now.'

NING WITH ANOTHER OF HER SPONSORS

'I'm coming! I'm coming!'

Tomas, the German, pounding Ning with his cock: 'You come for me, my little Thai sexpot. You come in buckets. You come for me, my baby.'

Ning and Tomas had arranged to meet months before. He was another of her sponsors. He was good that he was reliable like clockwork, not so good that he was not as generous as some of her others. The most he was sending her was twenty thousand baht a month. It was a fair amount, but Marco was sending thirty, Lee forty thousand and she could push it to sixty thousand. Then Lee had arrived in Pattaya unannounced. What the fuck was she gonna do now?

It's not easy being a Thai working girl with so many sponsors to juggle. But Ning was good at that. She knew how to cover her tracks. And was as wily as a fox. It was all about control, and convincing each gullible farang that he was the only one. It wasn't easy to do. These farangs, whether from the UK, USA, Australia, Europe, were intelligent men. They had good jobs, businesses, some were professionals, Doctors, Lawyers, Ex Military. Intelligent men, but when ensnared by a beautiful, exotic creature like Ning, all the intelligence seemed to go out of the window. She would lie and put on an act and tell a sob story about her family in Isaan being poor. And she'd touch that sensitive soft spot that all men have somewhere. Yes, seems incredible to some, but a half educated girl from rural Thailand had learned to wrap intelligent western men around her finger to the point that, when they go back to their own advanced country, they will send her money every month in the belief that they are the only one. You couldn't make it up.

Ning currently had five active sponsors. And that meant five different stories for them all. She kept in touch with them when they were in their own countries using Skype, Whatsapp and Line. It involved a variety of lies, including having separate ring tones for each one so she knew exactly who was calling her. And her lies even involved having a variety of different work clothes. You see, she had promised each one of them that, once she received her monthly money from them, she would no longer be a hooker, bar girl, freelancer. Instead, she made up a lie that she would work in a shop, a local convenience store. So, when she knew she would be getting a video call from one of her sponsors, she would quickly put on a work coat, with the distinctive name of the convenience store she lied about working in, and then accept the video call from her sponsor, whether he was in Germany, UK or wherever. A simple deception, but it worked wonders. The love struck farang on the other end would see her in her work clothes and think what a good girl, an angel, she was. This and other crafty deceptions Ning had got down to a tee.

But the important thing was not to let the farangs know about each other. In low season, March to November, this was easy because most of them didn't travel to Thailand at this time. It was the peak season months a girl had to be careful of, because they were all travelling out here then. And with Lee paying her a surprise visit when she had Tomas and Marco to attend with, it was troublesome.

The ironic thing was that Lee, a semi-skilled construction worker from Huddersfield, was the least educated out of them all, but the most generous sponsor. That's why she didn't want to lose him. She knew she'd have to think of something.

HOTEL RECEPTION

SEX TOURISTS NOT WELCOME says the sign.
Mr Choo was at reception talking to Pie. 'Do they have a problem paying that joiner fee?'

Pie: 'Some of them moan and complain about it. I just show them the sign and tell them they are lucky we allow them in.'

Mr Choo: 'That's good. 500 baht joiner fee seems reasonable.'

It was another bright morning at the Golden Thai hotel and the new arrivals were coming today. The hotel didn't just cater for ageing farangs and their Thai hookers, they also had couples and families. So the SEX TOURISTS NOT WELCOME sign was a necessity. The hotel still allowed guys to bring girls back, so long as they got a cut out of it.

The doors to reception swung open and the new arrivals came in. There were four of them, two women, two men, two separate double rooms.

The new arrivals approached the reception with their luggage. Pie gave her friendly Thai smile. 'Good morning, do you have a reservation here?'

A short, slight man spoke: 'Yes, Mr and Mrs Bale and Mr and Mrs Jones.'

Pie looked at the computer. 'Ahhh, you stay here two weeks.'

The two husbands looked a lot more cheerful than the two women. It was noticeable to Pie. She guessed the men were keener on Thailand than the women were. She wasn't far wrong.

'Look, Lizzy, we've got a view of the sea.'

Lizzy went to join her husband on the balcony. She grunted. 'Yeah, it's okay,' she said, unenthusiastically. She went back to unpacking her luggage.

George Bale went to the fridge and opened a beer. He was beaming. After that long journey from Birmingham he was so excited to be in Thailand. The heat alone was so welcoming after the freezing UK. 'I reckon, Lizzy, we have a quick shower and then get out on the town. We've got two weeks here and we may as well start tonight.'

Lizzy Bale, who, at twenty three stones was twice the bodyweight of her husband, continued sorting her stuff from the suitcases. Thailand, she thought. What the fuck was she doing here? And what was this holiday gonna be like? She and Carol had allowed the husbands to book the holiday this time. It was part of an agreement. After Lizzy and Carol's last holiday, a girls holiday to Gambia, George and Jeff had said they can only go if the next holiday was in Thailand. And they had all agreed.

And now they were here. And George and Jeff seemed a lot happier than their wives. Lizzy didn't have a good feeling about this.

Next door, Carol and Jeff were on their balcony. 'Lovely view,' Jeff said as he drank his first beer. 'God, I'm so glad I'm here. This is gonna be good.'

Carol looked glum. She drank a cola, not in a celebratory mood. She liked the view from the hotel balcony, but not the set up. How did Lizzy allow George and Jeff to dictate their holiday? Carol thought they had an ulterior motive. She's heard about all the slags in Thailand and ain't it funny that this is the place they had wanted to come to. Carol and Lizzy hadn't wanted to come here. They wanted their girls holiday to Gambia, which they'd been to many times, where they could shag loads of virile young black men and then go home and tell their husbands they had been lying on the beach all the time.

And now here they were in Pattaya, a scabby looking place in Thailand. The four of them. Two weeks stuck here in this fucking hole. This wasn't going to be a holiday, Carol decided. This was a fucking prison sentence.

JACK, KENNY AND LEE

After a couple of nights on the town, Jack and Kenny were now used to Lee being around. He seemed a bit pathetic at first. A gullible forty something farang who thought he'd met the girl of his dreams when the reality was very different. Ning was still not answering his calls and by now he had his suspicions about her. Jack and Kenny had wised him up and told him to stop looking for her and stop sending her money. Lee would probably do the second one, but the first one wouldn't be easy. She had made an impression on him that wouldn't go away any time soon.

Things were good in Pattaya. Jack, Kenny and Lee were having good nights and good days. Pattaya is a place where you're never short of female company, so long as you spend the dosh. This was November and peak season was beginning. There were plenty of girls around and an increasing number of farangs. Pattaya was busy and almost all the bars were lively with girls and music and the occasional money flush farang ringing bells and buying all the girls a drink. Some even rang the bell to buy everyone in the bar a drink. Pattaya is a fun place to spend your hard earned money.

'Why don't you get yourself a bird, Lee?' Kenny said to Lee when they were in a lively bar in Soi Boomerang. Jack and Kenny had a couple of tasty Thai birds on hand and were buying lady drinks and all that. They were both on for the night.

Lee, shook his head: 'Nah, not in the mood just yet.' He was still on the lookout for Ning, as if she'd miraculously appear.

Jack and Kenny were having a good time. In spite of the rise in prices, bar fines, lady drinks and everything else that goes with it, Pattaya was still the place to be.

Jack, squeezing a Thai bar girl close to him: 'This is great. So glad we came here again.'

Kenny: 'I'm starting to realise how good this place can be without the other clowns.'

Jack nodded: 'I'm with you on that one. Thank fuck we haven't got the other clowns.'

CHAPTER TWO

THE RETURN OF THE OTHER CLOWNS

The Emirates flight tore through the night sky on the second part of its journey bound for Bangkok. The lights had been dimmed. It was that moment in a flight when the food had been served and it was time for the passengers to get some sleep. It was night time, and the flight from Manchester to Bangkok was somewhere over India.

On board a tall, lean man had his eyes on the air hostesses. He had already had three included beers and wanted another. His economy seat was uncomfortable, especially since the selfish twat in front had put his seat back. The tall man did the same. Now where were those air hostesses? He'd noticed they were quite tasty and the thought of joining the mile high club...wow, what a start to the trip that would be. Come on, get one of them over here and start chatting her up. Wait a minute, they were muslims, weren't they? Or something like that. Well, what the fuck, he was sure some of them must be up for a shag.

One of the air hostesses, a dark, good looking one with a sexy body, passed by and he stopped her. 'Hey, I need another beer.'

The air hostess shook her head and said, 'Sorry, sir, we are out of beer.'

'Ohhhh, what...? I need a beer to sleep.'

She recognised him. He was the one making a nuisance of himself earlier. 'You already had beer, sir. Three, is it?'

'Well I want another.' He grinned his most handsome smile. 'Unless, you want to help me sleep.'

The air hostess grimaced. 'What do you mean by that, Sir?'

He looked into her dark, Arabic eyes. She was a fine looking young woman, that's for sure. He fancied something a bit exotic right now. 'How about it? Come on, I know you like me.'

The Air Hostess frowned, not sure what she was hearing. The tall man leaned closer and his grin broadened. 'How about you and me joining the Mile High Club?'

The air hostess gave him a look of thunder. 'No more beer, Sir. Go to sleep.'

She walked on by, leaving him disgruntled. Oh, well, he thought, if you don't try you never know.

He switched the overhead reading light on and took out his copy of the Bible. He was at the part where Jesus was feeding five thousand people with a tub of fishes. Some good stories in this, he decided.

FOUR MONTHS EARLIER
North Wales.

The gleaming white BMW sped through the rural roads of North Wales. It was a warm summer early evening and there were five men on board. One of them, the terrified man in the back, wished he had never gotten into the car.

'I think we are being followed,' the driver said. 'Don't turn around.'

The other men in the car glanced at the mirrors. Yes, it was a police car that was following them.

'What the fuck do they want?' the front passenger said. Then he thought. 'If they stop us I'll do the talking.' He wasn't the driver, but he didn't trust the other, big, suited men to talk to any Coppers. They may say the wrong thing. And there was that gibbering piece of shit they had trapped in the back that may start squealing. This wasn't good, Freddy decided.

The police car continued to follow the BMW for a few miles through the rural roads of North Wales, and then the predictable happened. It got up close behind them and indicated for them to pull over.

'Bastard!' Freddy Gibson, the big man in the front passenger seat, said. He then turned to his captive in the back. He gave Joey a cold, evil stare. 'You keep quiet, okay? You're in enough shit as it is. If you squeal it'll be the end for you. Okay?'

The terrified man in the back, trapped between two of Freddy Gibson's big, suited henchmen, nodded in fear.

The BMW pulled over in a lay-by and the police car stopped behind. Two uniformed officers, a man and woman, got out of the police car and approached them.

'Is this your car, Sir?' the red bearded copper said to the driver.

'No, it's mine.' Freddy Gibson said.

'And you are, Sir?'

'Freddy Gibson, Liverpool property Company. I own this car and this is my driver.'

'Can I see your driver's licence, Sir?' the copper said to the driver. The driver took out his licence and the police officer studied it. 'And what is your business in North Wales today, Sir?'

Freddy Gibson glared at the red bearded copper. Little shit, I could strangle him with my bare hands, Freddy thought. 'Tourism.'

The copper handed the licence back to the driver. 'Tourism? You come from Liverpool, yes? You come to North Wales as a tourist?'

Freddy: 'That's up to me. Now if you've finished we'll be on our way.'

Copper: 'We are not quite finished just yet, Sir?'

The male copper was approached by the female who said something to him. Freddy knew what she had said. This car was registered to him and his name was known to the police. He had been accused of being involved with County Lines and the police in Liverpool had stopped him a few times. He didn't figure the Welsh police would have his car on the computer as well.

The red bearded officer looked into the back of the car. He could see another three men. Two more suited men, and one in the middle who looked terrified. There had to be a reason for that. But this could be drugs related, and the police may have stumbled on something good here.

'Could you step out of the car, Sir?' the copper said to the driver. 'I need you to open the boot.'

The driver stepped out of the car. Freddy Gibson, the leader of the crew, did also. He didn't trust the driver to talk to the police. The driver could easily get violent. Freddy needed to keep things cool.

The two big men and the bearded copper went to the rear of the vehicle and opened the boot. The copper began fumbling around, hoping to find something good. Meanwhile, the female police officer turned her attention to the three men in the back. The one in the middle stood out as not being one of their crew. He was dressed casually, not wearing a suit like the others. And his expression was noticeably terrified. He clearly had something to hide.

'Can I ask you three men in the back to step out of the car, please?' she said.

The terrified man in the back of the car knew this was it. It had to be the moment. It was his one chance to save himself. It was now or never.

The two big, suited men in the back looked at each other. It wasn't wise to get out. They hesitated.

'I have to ask you to step out of the vehicle, gentlemen.', the female officer said. Still no response. 'Can you step out, please?' There was nothing of interest in the boot of the car so the driver closed it. Freddy Gibson looked into the face of the red bearded copper. A face he'd like to pulverise. 'So you won't be needing any more from us,' Freddy said. It wasn't a question.

Freddy and the driver were about to get back into the car and drive away when the female officer said, 'These three men are refusing to get out of the car. I've asked them twice but they are ignoring me.'

Come on, the frightened man thought. He was tense and sweating from the ordeal. This was his one chance, his one chance, his one chance to escape.. Come on, tell them to get out of the car....

The male police officer opened the rear passenger door and said, abruptly, 'Step out of the car, please, Gentlemen. That's an order.'

The big man nearest the door took great umbrage. He got out of the car abruptly and stared down at the two police. His expression was one of outrage. 'What the fuck is your problem, then, eh?' he blurted at the male officer, who stepped back in fear of an attack. The aggressive act was enough for the female to speak into her radio and call for reinforcements.

'Don't be aggressive, Sir,' the red bearded police officer said. 'No need for that.'

The big, suited man stared into the officer's face. 'Aggressive? I'll show you what aggressive is all about. Now FUCK OFF!'

Freddy Gibson was afraid of this. His henchmen were headstrong and could easily get violent. He stepped in to diffuse the situation.

I can't wait any longer, the man in the middle seat thought. I can't wait for this gorilla next to me to get out. I got to make a move now. Right now!

And in one move the frightened man undid his seatbelt and quickly moved across the back seats. And then he was out of the car. The frightened man stood before the police officers, unable to speak, but his appearance out of the car seemed to disturb everyone. The police looked at him, wondering who he was. The suited men looked at him, not knowing what he was going to do or say. And then Freddy Gibson, infamous Liverpool gangster, looked at him and said, 'Get back in the car, Joey. This has got nothing to do with you.'

You're damn right it hasn't, Joey thought. And with that, he ran. He ran fast, into a field. He ran as fast as he could, and he was a Marathon runner who could outrun most people. He heard voices behind him, alarmed voices, shouting for him to stop. But he didn't stop. He had to run for his life. So he ran and ran and soon was over the field and into another field. His arms started to bleed from being cut by hedges, but he didn't have time to stop. He had to run faster than he'd ever done in any race he'd been in. And then he was running down a lane past villages and people, and he ran down little alleyways and kept running until he was out of sight and range of everyone involved in that incident. He kept running. And he ran so far and for so long that nightfall eventually came. And it was only then that he stopped running. And he stopped, breathless and dripping with sweat. Hiding behind a shed, with the noise of animals. He could hear cows and other noises. And then he realised he was in a farmyard, somewhere in Wales.

'What are you doing, son?'

Joey looked up from behind the shed. His nostrils were filled with the smells of a farmyard. Then a light was shone in his face. Oh, no, oh no, who was this? Am I safe yet?

Joey stood up to face an old man with a deep Welsh accent.

'What are you doing here?' the old man said. 'This is my farm.'

Joey didn't know what to say or do. He was frightened, exhausted, lost, terrified, confused…He looked into the face of the old farmer. It was night time and the only light was from the man's torch. The old man continued to stare at him. Joey didn't know what to say. All he knew was he needed help. So Joey did something that was uncharacteristic of him, but he felt it was the only thing he could do. He broke down in tears and sobbed with his head in his hands.

The old man was joined by his wife and they both put their sympathetic hands on Joey's shoulders. 'It's alright, son,' the farmer said. 'Don't worry. You're safe now.'

Joey heard what the farmer said. You're safe now…Did he really say that? Am I safe now?

The old couple led Joey's sobbing, shivering body into the farmhouse and sat him down in a big chair. He did as he was told. He needed help badly and this old couple were the only ones offering any right now. He decided to play the game, whatever the game was.

The old couple cooked an evening meal in their cosy farmhouse kitchen. They told Joey to have a bath and put on some fresh clothing, which he did. This was good. They hadn't suggested anything about calling the police or a doctor or anything. They were most hospitable and he wanted to stay with them in safety as long as he could. He had nowhere else to go.

Joey was so uplifted when the old man said, 'It doesn't matter what you're running from, Joey. We don't need to know about that. It's a harsh world out there and we are here to offer you comfort for as long as you like. You'll be safe here, no harm will come to you. You make yourself at home, son.'

Joey was gobsmacked. As he sat at a dinner table eating with this old Welsh farming couple he thought they were the kindest people he had ever met. They were not his people, but he suddenly felt he wanted them to be. He wanted to be a part of their home. All his life he had met bastards so he needed to be a bastard himself to survive in a bastard place. But these here, this wonderful old couple, were not bastards. They were something different, a world apart from the one he'd known. And as he sat in their kitchen eating dinner with them, he felt so safe, as if the threats of the day were behind him.

Joey decided he had become a changed man. He would no longer be an Owlarse.

'Sir, is everything okay?' Joey opened his eyes to see an Arabic looking man staring as him. He had fallen asleep in his airplane seat and now he was woken by this flight attendant.

Joey nodded. What did this guy want?

'Sir, I have received a complaint about you.'

Joey's eyes widened. 'What about? From who?'

'My colleague. The girl who served you earlier. She said you have been making rude suggestions to her.'

Joey shuffled uneasily in his seat. 'Rude suggestions? Such as what?'

Attendant: 'You mentioned the Mile High Club to her, Sir. That is not allowed. You should not make comments like that to staff.'

Joey grinned: 'Well what should I say? It was only a joke. It's not as if I grabbed her tits or anything, is it?'

Attendant: 'This flight calls for a level of behaviour, Sir. And that is not acceptable.'

Joey: 'Then just get me another beer and I'll be happy.'

Attendant, realising this wasn't working: 'Are you from Liverpool, Sir?'

Joey: 'Yes. What's that got to do with anything.'

Attendant, smiling: 'I am a big fan of Liverpool. They are my favourite team.'

Joey: 'Good for you. Up the Reds.'

Attendant: 'Yes, come on the Reds.'

The mention of football diffused the situation, to both men's relief.

Attendant: 'Look, Sir, seeing as you are from Liverpool, we will forget about the incident. I'll get you another beer.'

Joey grinned and shook the guys' hand.

Attendant: 'You must realise, Sir, if you were Manchester United it would be a different story.'

The two men smiled at each other. Joey thought how amazing football could be. It could even make friends in a tricky situation. He'd wait for his beer and then go back to sleep.

Two rows behind Joey, his friend, another man from Liverpool, was fast asleep.

TWO DAYS EARLIER
Liverpool, England

I can't do this anymore, he thought as he sat in his rented taxi on the rank. It was night time and there was no one around, just the flashing lights of night time in the city. There's no future here for me, he decided. I got to do something.

Vinnie had heard about the others going back to Pattaya. It

was Autumn and business on the taxis was getting dire and the weather was getting colder and SouthEast Asia was the place to be for the month of November. The others were going there and he felt he had to go. He hated where he was right now and he had to be in Thailand again. He had only scratched the surface of Pattaya last time but he knew he would do better this time. He had to go there with his mates. He had to find a way to get out there. Except....

Vinnie had no money.

Vinnie was now 39, had been a taxi driver since his 20s, divorced with two children and an ex missus who thought he was a colossal pain in the arse. In fact, everyone eventually came to see Vinnie as a pain in the arse. Technically homeless, he had spent the years since his divorce dossing in other people's homes and outstaying his welcome. And his addiction to wacky baccy meant he could never save money. Massively in debt and potless, any money he earned from taxi driving either got spent on ganja or his two kids, who he still saw sporadically. Some taxi drivers can earn a decent amount of money, others never have anything to show for it. Vinnie was an extreme example of the second type.

So now it was November and Vinnie was sitting in his rented taxi on the ranks in a quiet corner of Liverpool. He hadn't had a fare for over an hour and wondered if he was going to be able to fill up the car before handing it back to the owner at the end of the night. He didn't want to be here. It was cold and depressing. And when he heard Jack and Kenny were heading to Thailand again....well, that just made him feel so bad. So jealous. So wishing he could save money like other people can.

And then Vinnie had an idea. It was a long shot, but it just might work. And the more he thought of it, the more he visaged sunny climates and hot massage girls ahead.

Two days later, Vinnie was baby sitting at his ex wife's house. It wasn't that unusual. He and his ex wife were still on friendly terms and it was a way for Vinnie to spend a bit of time with his two kids, a boy eight and a girl, ten.

It was Friday night and his ex wife was out with her boyfriend. He was some privileged twat who Vinnie didn't like. One of those 'I'm better than you are' types. Vinnie didn't care, as long as the twat stayed away from his kids.

So the two children were watching TV, a monster movie, Gorgo or something like that. And Vinnie needed a spliff. So he went outside to the yard and lit up a spliff. He smoked and thought for twenty minutes. And he thought about Jack and Kenny. Out there in Pattaya. Having the time of their lives. And he was stuck here miserable.

You must do it, Vinnie, this is your chance. It's now or never.

Vinnie finished his spliff and went back into the living room to check on the kids again. They were still watching the movie. Good. Now to make a move.

Vinnie went upstairs to his wife's bedroom.

It was a nice house. She was always very house proud and kept it clean and homely. Vinnie had fucked everything up with her. It was all water under the bridge now, but at least they still spoke and she lets him see the kids once a week.

Vinnie went into his ex wife's bedroom. He didn't need to look around. He knew where everything was. So he went over to the cabinet and opened the drawers. After fumbling about for a couple of minutes, he found what he was looking for. It was the jewellery box.

He opened the box and looked with awe at the goodies. He stopped to think for a moment about what he was doing. He reminded himself that he wasn't going to take anything that belonged to her. Only the stuff bought during their marriage.

He looked at his reflection in the mirror and reminisced about how things once were. When they were younger, he had his own taxi business and a marriage and a mortgage. And they were both earning money and life was good. So good they could even have the luxuries of jewellery, watches and rings, things he couldn't even dream about in his current poverty stricken state. And then it had all ended. It was his fault. His ganja addiction, his laziness, his inability to pay bills, his debt, his bankruptcy. She had been the one to find the money to keep hold of this house, but she ended the marriage. She'd had enough of his deviant ways. She branded him a loser and threw him out. And she kept the kids. Now she had a good life. She had a good job, two lovely children, a lovely house and a new boyfriend who had money. She had it made.

Vinnie had nothing. It was his own fault but it still made him bitter.

He observed closely the jewellery in the box. There were rings and necklaces and a ladies expensive watch which they had bought together. And there was also expensive jewellery that he hadn't even seen before. Jewellery that she had obtained since the divorce. But Vinnie had resolved to only take the stuff bought during their marriage. She had the house, didn't she? She had the kids, didn't she?

He looked at his reflection once again in the dim bedroom light and thought this was his way out. He was going to Thailand on a one way ticket, never coming back to this shit life again. He'd find something out there to keep going. Become an English teacher or something. He didn't want to come back here ever again. This jewellery was his plane ticket and money to get started. This was his passport to a better life.

He glanced at the jewellery in the box once again. He smiled at his reflection and then mumbled to himself, 'Fuck it. Just take the fucking lot.'

The following day Vinnie drove to a pawnbrokers in Manchester. He sold the jewellery for a handsome sum. Enough to get him started. Within a couple of hours he booked the ticket to Bangkok for the following day. His new life was soon to begin.

Now Vinnie slept as the plane tore through the night sky bound for Bangkok. Vinnie, without even thinking about it, had burned his bridges. After stealing the jewellery and leaving his ex wife's house, he suddenly realised what he had done. This was a serious offence, a police matter. But she couldn't prove it was him. And then, typical of Vinnie, he had a change of plan. Once his ex wife returned home he wanted to return some of the jewellery and just take what he had originally planned to take. But it was too late for a change of plan. And then he thought he may as well be ruthless and consider that she had everything that was once his. The least he could take was something to get him started in a new life. He'd already lost all that he could lose. What was done was done. And Vinnie now slept on a flight bound for Bangkok.

Two rows behind Vinnie sat two men who had recently become good friends. One of them was an old friend of Joey and Vinnie. The man sitting next to him was a newcomer to their friends circle. The two men had met each other quite recently, in the most unforeseen of circumstances.

THREE WEEKS EARLIER
A PSYCHIATRIC WARD IN LIVERPOOL

Pete had been sectioned. His behaviour had become so erratic that he was believed to be a danger to himself and others. He was diagnosed with Post-traumatic stress disorder.

He had taken a beating from his brother and other family members on his return home from Thailand. He had stolen his mother's bank card and squandered thousands of pounds of her money. His family wasn't going to let him get away with that. So they taught him a lesson once and for all. They gave him a damn good hiding, broken ribs included. Hospitalisation.

It had all come too much for Pete, who, a former University dropout, had lost his way in life. A colossal disappointment to the family who once had high hopes for him. And, after his own family had turned against him, it didn't end there. Just a week after leaving hospital, still bruised and bandaged, he strayed into the wrong pub in Liverpool and came face to face with an old friend who Pete had cheated out of money. The guy, who Pete had borrowed from and then done a runner, attacked and beat up Pete badly, sending him to casualty for the second time in a matter of weeks. Pete had had enough by now. He had a breakdown. Behaving in a way that they'd never seen before. Jumping out of upstairs windows, self harming himself, suicidal but couldn't carry it through. So his family had him sectioned and put in a mental ward. His family no longer cared for him, so the hospital could have him. Not their problem anymore.

Pete, a 30 year old with no longer any hope in life, spent months in the psychiatric ward. He had been taken away by the men in white coats. And the behaviour of people in there was crazy. He saw crazy behaviour, people shouting and crying for no reason, being wrestled to the ground by the security staff, people being put in straightjackets, defecating on the floor of the ward, and nutters climbing on his bed in the middle of the night. Was he himself now a nutter? Pete asked himself. He must be because he was here.

Pete had been discarded into this crazy environment, with no hope and no future. Pete now wanted to die. He just didn't have the guts to do it.

But at least Pete had made a new friend. His name was Billy. Known to those who knew him in his Liverpool area as, 'Basket Case Billy'.

'I just want to die, Billy,' Pete said as they sat next to each other on a settee, watching loonies wandering aimlessly about the ward. 'I just want to die.'

Billy: 'You shouldn't want to die, Peter. There's no future in that.'

Pete: 'But I have no future, Billy. I have no future.'

Billy: 'As long as you have me for a friend, you have a future.'

They were kind words of wisdom from a man whom others regarded as lunatic. And a highly dangerous one at that. Billy had spent most of his adult life in prison for violence, or threats of violence. He had a liking for swords and had waved them about in public too often. He was now under review and had been put in this psychiatric ward temporarily before being let loose on the world. Some said his behaviour had calmed. Others opposed his release saying it was only a matter of time before he killed someone.

Billy liked Pete. Pete was quiet and looked harmless and would listen to Billy's ramblings and was good company. In a world where good friends were hard to come by, Billy felt he'd made a friend out of this quiet, pleasant looking young man.

Pete however, didn't feel the same way about Billy. To Pete, Billy was a nutjob, a big, frightening looking man and his talk of carving people up with swords and stuff sent shivers down Pete's non violent spine. But Billy was what he had in this loony bin. Billy was the only friend who would listen to him. Billy was the only words of any comfort on offer right now.

'This is all his fault,' Pete said, looking around at the crazy people. Typically Pete blamed someone else for his problems. It was never his fault. It was not his fault that he had stolen his mother's bank card to go on holiday with Jack, Kenny, Joey and Vinnie. It was not his ,fault that he got beaten up by his brother on his return home. It was not his fault that his dire situation, a former college boy who didn't want to work ended up on sickness benefit. It wasn't his fault that his family had come to regard him as a loser. It wasn't Pete's fault that he had no money and was always borrowing to maintain a lifestyle that he simply hadn't worked for. It wasn't his fault that he'd had a breakdown, had attempted a half baked suicide and ended up in a loony bin. Pete never blamed himself for anything. It was always someone else to blame.

Billy: 'It's whose fault?'

Pete, looking down at the floor of a mental hospital ward. 'It's his fault.'

Billy: 'Who, Pete? Who, my friend? Whose fault is it that you've ended up here? Whose fault is it that you don't want to live any more? Is someone to blame for all this? You just tell me who it is, my friend?'

Pete continued staring blankly at the floor and then said, 'It's the Dutchman. It's his fault.'

Billy, his eyes widening after hearing a name: 'The Dutchman? Who is this Dutchman? Who is this man who has caused you to end up in a lunatic ward?'

Pete: 'His name is Michael. Michael the Dutchman.'

Billy felt his vengeful, violent nature rising. Michael the Dutchman. That's the bastard who has caused his friend to want to end his own life. Michael the Dutchman. Billy had a name. Billy now needed to know who is this Michael the Dutchman.

Billy: 'Who is this Michael the Dutchman? And where can I find him?'

Pete, continuing to stare at the floor: 'Pattaya. He's in Pattaya.'

Billy: 'Pattaya? Where? Where is this Pattaya?'

Pete then put his head in his hands and sobbed. He sobbed his heart out while he told Basket Case Billy of that terrifying time in Pattaya when he had been kidnapped and tied to a bed while SM weirdos stood around and watched him being violated by ladyboys. And he was chained, like an animal, and forced onto a stage where he was whipped and about to be buggered by ladyboys. And he told Billy of that sly, sly bastard who owned that club and had instigated it all for the sick pleasure of weirdos. And he thought about what would have happened to him if his mates hadn't come to the rescue. He cried and sobbed and sobbed so much his body shook. The tears ran freely as Pete sobbed his story out to his psycho friend in a ward full of loonies. This is what Pete's life had come to.

Basket Case Billy had heard enough. And it was shocking. And no one should get away with that. All as Billy knew was that Pete, this nice young Liverpool boy, was now a broken man. But at least Billy now had a name. A solid name and description he could target. Michael the Dutchman.

Billy, patting his sobbing friend on the back: 'Don't worry, Pete, my friend. It will all come good again. There is nothing that cures a broken man more than wreaking vengeance on the evil man who caused it. And that is exactly what we shall do. I'm out of here soon, and then we'll go there together. You and me will go to this Pattaya place. And we'll seek out the man who done you wrong. And we will wreak the most horrible vengeance upon this man. Michael the Dutchman. We'll make this man sorry for the day that he was born. Because, Pete, you are now my friend. And no one, no one does this to a friend of mine.'

Billy sat back in his seat as his friend continued to sob his heart out. Billy felt uplifted because he now had a goal. A mission. Something solid to aim for. And then Billy's face cracked into a sinister smile and he said to himself, 'There's nothing I like better than a good murder.'

CHAPTER THREE

PATTAYA DOES NOT APPEAL TO EVERYONE

'Hi, Guys, this is Lenny Pazzaz and his trusty terrier sidekick Seamus, bringing you another round up of what's happening in the sun soaked, naughty but nice seaside paradise called Pattaya.'

Lenny Pazzaz settled in his chair for another two hour live extravaganza from his bar in Soi 13. It was now his regular Friday night slot and drew in a thousand viewers per show. Not a record, but for his modest Youtube channel it was pretty good. And it was a good way of drawing customers to his bar. The Youtube channel and the girly bar worked well together. Customers from UK, America and beyond watched his show live and then dropped into his bar when they came to Pattaya. They spent money on the girls, he was happy, the girls were happy, everyone was happy. Well, almost everyone. Seamus, his grumpy sidekick co host, wasn't always happy but they kind of worked well together.

Seamus, regardless of what others thought, didn't dislike Lenny. He just found him a bit annoying. Lenny, you see, had been a local radio DJ in Sheffield many years ago but his failure in life was that he'd never hit the big time. Lenny tried to join the BBC in the 1990s, only to be rejected because his cheesy style was very much 1970s. His style was old hat, his jokes were corny, even his wavy hairstyle looked like it belonged in the Glam Rock era. Lenny had grown up wanting to be a Radio 1 DJ but had missed the boat. Now, with a failed career, a failed marriage and a failed everything else behind him, he moved out of the

UK and made his home in Pattaya. Now he had his own bar, his own Youtube channel and was surrounded by people who appreciated him. Not a passport to fame and fortune, but you can't have everything.

Seamus: 'So, on the show tonight we have our guest, Johnny Mason, who, as you know, is an expert on Pattaya and will be telling us all the latest news and what's going on here in Sin City. And, of course, we have some lovely ladies here for your viewing pleasure.'

There were plenty of lovely Thai girls in the bar. Lenny had to be careful about some of the girls who got a bit raunchy before the camera. This was Youtube, remember, and cleavage and arses were not advertiser friendly.

Seamus, bringing a Thai lady and her low cut top before the camera: 'And what's your name, then?'

'Pan,' the sexy Thai girl said.

Seamus, looking down at her tits: 'And what do you like most about being here on the Lenny Pazazz show?'

Pan, not speaking clear English: 'I like…drink…I like…men buy me drink…'

Seamus: 'You like men to buy you a drink? Yes, that's good. And if I was to buy you a drink, Pan, what would you do for me?'

Pan, grinning and flashing her cleavage at the camera: 'I like….fuck…I fuck you….'

Seamus, quickly pulling the microphone away and grimacing at the camera: 'You didn't hear that. If you are watching on Youtube you didn't hear that.'

Lenny Pazazz heard it and once again thought Seamus was deliberately winding him up. Lenny had already had complaints from Youtube and the last thing he needed was a busty Thai girl saying 'fuck' to the camera.

Lenny: 'Okay, apologies to any viewers who heard that. We'll edit that for the uploaded version later. In the meantime let me remind you that we have some very special guests lined up for the show in the coming weeks. Pattaya is having some great new go go bars opening for this season and we'll have some special guests here to tell us all about it.'

SOI CHAIYAPOON: A BRAND NEW LADYBOY SHOW BAR IS ABOUT TO OPEN

Soi Chayapoon, Pattaya, is affectionately known as Soi Pothole. No matter how many times the Thai authorities repair the road, sooner or later the potholes return. In spite of that, this is one of the liveliest Sois in the Soi Buakow area. Once mainly known for massage parlours, it now boasts a variety of bars, live band venues and even some upmarket Gentlemen's clubs. It is also to be the venue for a Ladyboy cabaret show bar about to open soon. The sign above the club says, 'NAUGHTY BOYS'.

Inside the club the owner was watching the Ladyboys rehearse. On the stage there were six Ladyboys, of good quality, and the Mamasan and a dance teacher were coaxing them on their moves. It was a shaky start, but after a couple of weeks of practice, they were getting there. In fact, everything was getting there. What helped enormously is that these Ladyboys had been carefully chosen by the owner himself. He needed quality, Ladyboys who had sang and danced before, could entertain the customers, weren't shy. The last thing he needed were a bunch of rookies. He needed this club to work, no setbacks. After his last disastrous venture he needed to get back on his feet at soon as possible.

It had been almost a year since his SM club had been closed down. He'd lost so much money, a financial disaster involving paying off shareholders and staff and all kinds of other messy garbage . And it was all because of those bastards from Liverpool. He knew they were from Liverpool because Vinnie was one of them. Vinnie, the stray who he'd taken in and looked after after being ostracised by his own friends. And then that Scouser boy Pete. The masked men had come to rescue him from the club, caused mayhem, chased out his customers, ruined his reputation amongst the SM network, even stole his expensive camera which he'd used to make porn movies for his shady website. He was doing so well, he had it made with that club. Those SM crowds were wealthy punters, and were bringing a fortune into that backstreet club. They were paying top dollar for the finest champagne, hiring Ladyboys for orgies and live sex shows and paying a premium for the privelidge. It was going great. But then, just one incident was all it took. A stray, a Scouser called Pete, had been dumped into the building having cheated a ladyboy out of money. It wasn't the first. He had an agreement with some ladyboys that they could kidnap a punter and get paid for it. The unfortunate guy would then be forced into a sex show before being drugged and tossed out into an alleyway somewhere. Served him right. But they had picked the wrong one. Pete had friends, including Vinnie, and the end result was carnage at the club. Police had come and closed the place down, part of a cleaning up of the area or some other bullshit.

Michael sat back in his chair and continued to watch the ladyboys rehearsing. He called over the dance coach.

Michael, in his Dutch accent: 'I am not liking it. It's too clean.'

Thai man: 'Too clean? How?'

Micheal, grinning: 'Tell them to lift their skirts up a bit more, show some dick. The customers want dirty shows. This place is called Naughty Boys. It has to live up to that.'

The Thai dance teacher nodded, and went back to the ladyboy troupe on the stage to give further instructions. It wasn't difficult to persuade these Ladyboys to be a bit more raunchy. They'd been at it for years and knew what the customers wanted. The show resumed with more dick on show.

Michael continued to watch a while longer, and then went into his office at the rear of the club. He sat at his desk and poured himself a coffee. He needed to think. It was just a week before the club was due to open and he wasn't getting the publicity he needed. Times were not hard in Pattaya, but they weren't easy, either. Lots of competition. He had chosen the Naughty Boys venue here in Soi Chaiyapoon because it was away from Boystown. Far too much competition there, and this would be ideaf for Soi Buakow customers who didn't want to go very far. Soi Chaiyapoon was very up and coming and his would be the first major Ladyboy cabaret show in the Soi. It couldn't fail. But he needed publicity. He'd already spent a bit on advertising but he needed more. The problem was that other bar owners were reluctant to give him any help. Michael was not popular amongst the community because of rumours of his shady past which involved prison in his native Netherlands. He'd always denied the rumours, but nevertheless many of the bar owners refused to entertain him.

There was, however, someone else who he could call on for help. A guy who he'd never had any dealings with but was now well known in the Pattaya entertainment community because of his Youtube live shows. Personally, Michael couldn't stand Lenny Pazazz. He'd seen him a couple of times in various bars and had watched a bit of his live shows. Michael had nothing against him personally, just found that annoying Seventies DJ persona to be as unbearable as his corny jokes. Yet, nevertheless, the Lenny Pazazz show was really gaining ground and got quite a large Youtube audience several times a week. And Lenny always seemed to be on the lookout for new guests.

Give it a go, Michael thought. He drank his coffee and checked his watch. It was getting towards evening. Another hour or so and he'd be paying Lenny Pazazz a visit. It was a long shot. Lenny didn't owe Michael anything. But Michael needed that publicity to get back on his feet, and, love him or hate him, Lenny Pazazz was the hottest Youtube live show in town.

JACK, KENNY AND LEE

Jack and Kenny had got off to a great start in Pattaya. The nights out were good, the girls were good, everything was good. And the fact that they had a new mate, Lee, was also good. He was a cool guy, if a bit naive. He'd splash the cash around in the bars in the way Jack and Kenny wouldn't. After a couple of days Jack could see why he had been a target for a devious Thai girl called Ning.

So they were having a night out in the Soi Buakow area. It was a nightlife area popular with farangs and expats with plenty going on without the expensive Walking Street prices.

And it was a great night in an area called LK Metro, an L shaped alleyway of bars, live bands, go go bars, kebabs and all the things you would want from a nightlife scene.

Jack had met a Thai bird who had become his regular. Her name was Bee and she was a nice bird, sexy but not in your face type. He met her in a reggae bar with a live band. She was the type of bird you couldn't go wrong with. So long as you observed the three day rule.

Kenny also observed the three day rule with his birds. Unfortunately, Lee was of a different sort. Wanted to fall in love and that sort of thing. He was good company, though, and Jack and Kenny liked having him around.

They were in a crowded bar and Lee suddenly got a text message. He seemed excited when he showed it to the lads. It was from Ning, and she wanted to meet him in a nearby bar.

Lee, his eyes widening as he read the message on his phone: 'Oh, My God, it's Ning! She's here. She's here in Pattaya. Oh, My God, my baby is here.'

Jack and Kenny looked knowingly at each other. They liked Lee, but he was acting more and more like a Simp.

Lee, excited: 'I got to go, lads. I got to go. She's in that little bar on the corner of Soi Honey. I know the one. I got to go and meet her. My Ning, my beautiful Ning.'

Lee headed along the busy Soi Buakow to a little bar where Ning said she was going to be. And there she was. Ning, sitting at a bar with another Thai girl, waiting for him. She looked amazing and he was so glad to see her.

'Ning, my love,' Lee said, embracing her. 'Where have you been?'

Ning, smiling: 'Lee, I have missed you. I had to go see family.'

There followed several minutes of huggy, huggy, kissy, kissy, soppy, sentimental stuff which, if Jack and Kenny had witnessed it, they would have either cringed with embarrassment or creased up with laughter.

Lee, sitting down at the table with Ning and her friend: 'Ning, I've so missed you. Why didn't you answer my messages.' He then thought that was a selfish question to ask, so decided to be more thoughtful. 'How is your family? How's your mum? Is she alright? Is everything okay?'

Ning looked down to the table: 'My Momma not well. She been ill. I had to go see her. I have to give her some money. Papa not well, either.'

Lee pulled a shocked expression: 'Oh, my darling, that's so bad. Oh, I hope they get better. Don't worry, dear, I'll help you. No problem.'

Ning, smiling at Lee's warm, generous heart: 'Oh, will you, Lee?' She put her arms around him and kissed him again. 'You are such kind man.'

Lee smiled at Ning, his love, and her Thai friend who sat quietly observing the romantic couple. 'I think we'd better start ordering some drinks.' And without waiting for a waitress to come over Lee got up and rang the bell to buy all the staff a drink. They all cheered the kind gesture from this man. He looked into Ning's beautiful eyes. 'Oh, my lord, I'm so happy to see you, my love. You don't know what you mean to me.'

Ning smiled softly: 'And you don't know what you mean to me, Lee.'

CAROL AND LIZZY

'It's shit here,' Carol said. 'It's fucking shit.'

Lizzy was munching on a sandwich as Carol was laying back on a sunbed at the hotel pool.

'Stop moaning,' Lizzy said with a mouthful of sandwich. 'We've only been here for two days. It'll get better.'

Carol: 'How's it gonna get better? These fucking Thai fellas are not interested in a couple of fat English women. They're so used to their little skinny birds. We're out of place here. If we were in Gambia we'd have shagged loads of fellas by now.'

Lizzy looked over to a Thai waiter, one of the better looking ones, who was serving drinks at the pool. Not even a glance from him. The fact that she was twice his bodyweight wouldn't have made any difference in Gambia or Turkey, another of their old haunts.: 'Keep your voice down. There's people listening.'

Carol: 'Who's listening? Most of them can't even speak English.'

Carol was pissed off. Lizzy was pissed off, too. The reason they were on this holiday was to placate their husbands. Carol and Lizzy had been going together to Gambia and Turkey for years on a girls holiday. Their dimwitted husbands had become suspicious and had insisted that the next holiday would be in Thailand. So they had ended up here. A couple of fat, middle aged English women in a hot, sweaty place infamous for men who like to shag young girls.

Lizzy: 'Look at that dirty old bastard over there.'

Carol, lifting her head from the sunbed: 'Who, that baldy old fella in his budgie smugglers?'

Lizzy, fuming: 'He's about sixty five and she's about twenty three.' Lizzy watched as the old farang put his arms around his young Thai girl in the bikini. 'Fucking pervert. And as for her, don't these young girls have any pride in themselves? I hope she fucking takes him for every penny he's got.'

Carol: 'You know, I had a dream last night. I dreamt I was in Turkey and I was being shagged by Ahmed. He was ramming me in every hole with his big Turkish cock. And then I woke up and I was here with that drunken fucker lying in bed next to me.'

Lizzy: 'I'm going for a swim in the pool.'

Carol, laughing: 'Don't dive in or you'll drain the pool out.'

Lizzy: 'Ha, fucking ha.'

Carol: 'By the way, where are those two fuckers? Where have they got to?'

SOI 6

'This place is well out of the way, they'll never catch us here.'

George and Jeff were on the Baht bus through Second road. The Baht bus was a great service. Just hop on for ten baht and you could be miles away, somewhere the wives will never catch you.

Jeff: 'I've heard great reviews for this street. Been so looking forward to it.'

George, looking at his map: 'I think we're coming up to it now.'

George and Jeff got off the baht bus and paid the driver through the window. They entered Soi 6 to see a long, narrow Soi brimming with girly bars on either side. They walked down the Soi and were greeted by Thai girls in skimpy clothes, mini skirts and bare flesh all around. Evey bar they passed had a dozen or so girls smiling at them, beckoning them inside.

Soi 6 was a great stalwart of Pattaya. Just when you thought you were heading out of town this infamous sexual playground pops up, and how? Brimming with bars with names like Foxy Chicks, Lusty Girls, you get the picture. Soi 6 was where you go for a drink and a quick shag, with short time rooms upstairs from the bars, all at a very reasonable price.

George, his eyes popping out at what he saw: 'Lizzy would kill me if she knew I was here.'

Jeff: 'Carol wouldn't be too pleased about it, either. Well, they're at the hotel and we are miles away.'

George: 'Just a thought, maybe that's why Soi 6 is so far away from the rest of the action. It's so husbands can go swanning off without their wives finding them.'

The bars were brilliant, with the sauciest of names, and the girls were HOT. George and Jeff were grinning. This looked as good as they'd heard.

Jeff, looking concerned: 'I hope none of these are those ladyboys things. I've heard about that. Don't want any dick and balls popping out.'

George: 'Nah, I think that's the back alley, Soi 6/1. That's where they hang out. I think they do have few ladyboys among this lot. I think the idea is to have a good feel before you do anything with them.'

Jeff: 'Well, so long as I don't get any of them up my back alley...'

'Hello,' a young Thai girl stepped out in front of them as they were walking past. She grabbed George's wrist. 'You come in bar.' She then stood closer to him. She was gorgeous, slender and young. 'We go upstairs and I do everything for you.'

George's eyes widened. He loved the sound of that. He turned to Jeff who was already being cajoled into the bar by another girl. George turned back to the sexy young Thai girl in the mini skirt. He was miles away from his wife. She'll never find him here.

George, looking into the Thai girl's eyes: 'Okay. Lead the way.'

CHAPTER FOUR

JACK AND KENNY FACE DANGER

Ning wrapped her legs around Lee. They were in bed together in Lee's hotel room. Lee rolled on his back. It was morning and his head ached from the night before.

Ning, stretching her arms out and rubbing her eyes: 'Mmmmm, I so glad you are back, Lee. I so miss boom boom with you.'

Lee: 'You miss our boom boom? And you haven't boom boomed with anyone else since you last saw me?'

Ning, frowning: 'No. No, no, I no boom boom with anyone but you. Why you think that?'

Lee: 'Well, you didn't answer my calls or texts so I just thought…..Oh, I didn't know what to think. Anyway, enough of that, you're here now. And we've had a good night. That's all that matters.'

Yes, they'd had a good night. Lee was so thrilled to see Ning again. He'd been with her on three previous visits to Pattaya and she was the girl he wanted to take back to England. He was generous with her, sending her 40K baht per month. But she wanted more, she wanted 60k a month. Lee would pay that to look after her. But was she sincere? And, by the way, the money didn't end there, either. Ning, like most Thai girls, had a family in Isaan, the rural area of Thailand where most Thai bar girls come from. She had Mum, Dad, two brothers and a sister. And they all needed money. Marry a Thai girl and you marry the whole family. You, as a supposed wealthy farang, are the one expected to cough up the dough when it was needed.

And some of these girls and their families could bleed you dry. Whether it was a new motorbike for her brother or help with her father's business, the farang is expected to pour money down a bottomless pit.

But Lee wasn't concerned about that. All he knew is he was smitten with Ning and wanted to be with her permanently. Jack and Kenny thought he was naive, but didn't know him well enough yet to tell him so.

Lee was from Huddersfield, in Yorkshire. He was forty two years old and worked as a bricklayer and other odds jobs. He was hard working, could even earn a decent wage, and Huddersfield, a traditional market town close to the Pennines, was not a bad place to live. But Lee didn't have a good life there. He was married once and his wife took him to the cleaners, taking the house that he had worked hard for for years, leaving him in an expensive rented flat. Since then he had become disillusioned with English women. He'd had his fingers burned, it had cost him dearly. And it made him laugh when people said to watch out for those Thai girls, they'll take all your money. Lee's experience was that English women will do exactly the same thing. His wife took him to the cleaners, a Yorkshire girl who he'd known since school and had trusted. And after the divorce, with Lee left with virtually nothing, what added insult to injury was the sight of his ex-wife swanning around town in a sports car with her handsome new boyfriend. Lee wasn't violent, but he felt like strangling her whenever he saw her out and about, gloating at him as she passed by. Fucking bitch.

So Lee didn't think there was anything unusual about a Thai girl wanting money from a bloke. And, of course, there was another reason he was besotted with her. The sight of her walking naked around his hotel room, that perfectly lean and shapely dusky skinned body and her beautiful, exotic face. Ning was gorgeous. She was worth taking a chance on.

After they got out of bed, Ning and Lee dressed and went downstairs.

Lee: 'Let's go to Soi Buakow. There's some nice restaurants there. It's too late for breakfast so we'll have dinner together.'

Ning, shaking her head: 'No, we go somewhere else.'

Lee: 'Why? I thought you liked Soi Buakow.'

Ning: 'No, we go Soi 8. There nice cafes there.'

Lee: 'Okay, we'll get a taxi there.'

They spent the day together and Lee was happy, happier than he'd been since arriving in Pattaya. Ning knew she had to be careful. There were people she just didn't want to run into, especially in the company of Lee. It could all end in tears.

JACK AND KENNY

They were four days into the holiday and Jack and Kenny were having a great time. They'd had girls, plenty of booze and no problems. Pattaya at its best. Couldn't ask for better.

So they were sitting at a familiar bar complex on beach road having an afternoon beer. Kenny was chatting away to a Thai waitress. He bought her a drink and she was rubbing her cleavage in his face as a thankyou. Jack, meanwhile, was staring out to sea, in a reflective mood. This was good here, he thought. Maybe too good. He was always suspicious of anything that was too good. But to be here in the month of November, in blazing heat, shorts and T-shirt, away from the depressing cold of the UK, was quite wonderful. He'd worked hard for this holiday, and it was great to be enjoying it and being far more relaxed than last time when he had the other clowns to contend with.

Kenny, swigging his beer: 'I'm gonna wear my fucking dick out before I leave here. So many hot chicks about.'

Jack, nodding: 'Yeah. I was just thinking, could you do this forever? I mean, if you could afford to retire here do you think you could just shag Thai birds every day until your dick drops off?'

Kenny downed his beer and grinned: 'Yes.'

Jack, shrugging: 'I'm not so sure. I mean, I reckon the novelty could wear off after a while. Like working in a sweet shop. After a while you don't bother touching them.'

Kenny: 'I dunno, I've had some sexy little chicks since I've been here. It would take something for me to get tired of them.'

Jack: 'But shagging different girls night after night, with no end to it. It becomes, well…not the real world.'

Kenny, grimacing at how deep in thought his mate was: 'Not the real world? You're kidding. I tell you what, if the real world is living in a miserable suburb of Liverpool doing a depressing building job in the freezing cold and then going to to the same old shitty pubs on a weekend, well, you can keep it. If that's the real world, give me this one anyday.'

Jack nodded: 'Yeah, suppose you're right.'

Truth was, Jack was thinking of Minnie, the Thai bird he'd been with last time and had taken to the island of Koh Samet. She seemed the perfect girl for him. Until he began getting paranoid over her constant obsession with her mobile phone. Jack didn't trust anyone and, sadly, that came to include Minnie. He still hoped he could see her again.

Like any country which is popular with tourists, Thailand is not free of scams. Thailand is not the worst offender for scams, but, nevertheless, they do exist. And no matter how much common sense and precaution you exercise, a scam can appear out of nowhere when you least expect it. This happened to Jack and Kenny when they were heading into town early evening and decided to have a quick beer in a nice cosy little bar in Soi 7.

There were no other customers in the bar and Jack and Kenny had been coaxed in by a friendly looking young Thai man with long hair and tattoos. It was a rock bar and the music was good so they went in to have a quick drink to start the night. They sat at a wooden table and ordered Heinekens. The bar was appealing, with pictures of Hendrix, Morrison and the Stones on the walls. The young man, who looked like a solidly built Thai boxer, came over to chat to them at the table.

Thai man: 'Where are you from? You Irish?'

Jack: 'No, close. Liverpool.'

Thai man: 'Ahhh, Liverpool. I like Liverpool football.'

Jack: 'I prefer the Beatles. They were actually from Liverpool.'

Thai man: 'Ahhhh, Beatles, is good. I like the Beatles.' Then he had a thought. 'I can play Beatles songs. Let me show you.'

The Thai man went behind the bar and reappeared at their table with a small, Asian looking guitar. He pulled up a chair close to them and began to play a few chords. Not very well. It sounded a bit like Yesterday. If his guitar playing was bad enough it got worse when he started to sing.

Jack and Kenny looked at each other and grinned. This was not the kind of entertainment they were looking for, but they humoured him. After a few minutes of musical torture, the Thai man put the little guitar on on the floor, leaning it upright on the the leg of the table. He went back to the bar to check his mobile phone.

Jack and Kenny sat at the table drinking their Heinekens. Jack looked at the little guitar and thought it had been placed precariously by the Thai man. Then, from a slight movement by Kenny at the table, the guitar fell over and a wooden panel fell off it. The Thai man exclaimed something and came rushing over to the table. 'What happened?' he said in alarm. Jack and Kenny shrugged. Then the Thai man picked up the guitar and pulled out the panel which had come loose. His face looked alarmed and he said, 'Oh, fuck, it's broken!'

Jack, sensing something devious here. 'How is it broken?'

Thai man, showing him the panel which had come loose: 'Here. This is hand made guitar, very expensive. It must be repaired.'

Kenny, also sensing something devious here: 'Well, you're the one who left it leaning against a table leg.'

Thai man: 'Oh, no, Sir. It only broke when you moved table. You must pay for damage.'

Kenny: 'WHAT! I'm not paying for any damage. That's your fucking guitar and you left it leaning against a dodgy table.'

Thai man: 'Oh, no, don't get angry, Sir. It's very expensive guitar. No problem when I left it here. Only broken when you moved table.'

Jack looked angrily at the Thai man, and then to Kenny: 'Careful, Ken, this is a scam.'

The Thai man overheard Jack and shook his head. 'No, scam, Sir. You must pay for damage.'

Two other Thai men, young and muscular like the bar man, appeared in the doorway. They entered and immediately went to the table. One of the Thai men picked up the guitar, looked it over and said something to the others. Jack and Kenny were now faced with three Thai men, who all looked like they could have a go. This was bad.

Jack downed the rest of his beer. It was time to go. He pulled out two hundred baht which would cover the beers for him and Kenny and put it on the table. 'Drink up, Kenny, it's time to leave.'

Thai man: 'You must pay for damage, Sir.'

Jack, angrily: 'We didn't cause any damage. You left that guitar next to the table.'

'Five thousand baht,' said one of the other Thai men. 'It's handmade and will need to be repaired.'

Thai man: 'Yes, five thousand baht and we will forget about it.'

Jack looked at the three young, muscular Thai men. They were all grinning. They had done this scam before. He was angry but the odds were stacked against him and Kenny.

Kenny, standing up belligerently: 'FUCKOFF! Is this one of your regular fucking scams is it?'

The three Thai men stood close together. These were rough boys, and this wasn't gonna end well for the two Englishmen.

Jack, rising more calmly from his chair: 'Look, we all know your little game. You left that guitar there deliberately and there is no way that's five thousand baht of damage. The fucking guitar isn't worth that much. Now give it a rest, will you. There's two hundred for the drinks, now goodbye.'

Jack and Kenny attempted to walk out but the Thai men blocked their path and had aggressive looks on their faces. This could turn ugly.

Jack: 'Get out of our way! You are not dealing with dummies here. We will call the police.'

The Thai men laughed: 'Call the police?' one of them said. 'The police will arrest you! You will join other drunken farangs in jail.'

Kenny: 'Fuck off! The lot of you fucking pricks can just fuck off. Now get out of our way.'

Jack and Kenny had no other ideas other than to physically barge past the three Thai men, but it wasn't wise. What followed was a couple of minutes of standoff, shoving from both sides, Jack being manhandled by two of them and Kenny squaring up to the Thai barman who had caused it all. Kenny was about to throw a punch when, miraculously, a voice came from nowhere and bellowed:

'WHAT THE FUCK IS GOING ON HERE!?'

Jack turned. Kenny turned. The Thai men turned to see a big, sturdy, aggressive looking farang with threatening eyes and a malicious grin. 'WHAT THE FUCK IS GOING ON HERE?' he repeated. Jack and Kenny noticed he was aiming his aggression towards the three Thai men. They also noticed he had a Liverpool accent, like them.

It took Jack and Kenny a few confused seconds to consider who this man was. And then, the last thing they could possibly ever have expected, they looked toward the doorway. Three other men stood there, watching what was going on.

Kenny's mouth dropped open.

Jack's mouth dropped open.

Kenny: 'Joey!'

Jack: 'Vinnie!'

Kenny: 'Pete!'

Jack: 'What the f......'

The Thai barman who had caused all this turned to Jack. 'You know these men?'

Kenny: 'Yes, we fucking do. And it looks like you're outnumbered.'

'What is happening here?' the big man said as Joey, Pete and Vinnie, their old mates from Liverpool, came to stand behind him. 'I want an explanation.'

The Thai men looked lost for words, perturbed by this unexpected intrusion. Scared, even, realising the boot could now be on the other foot.

Jack, to the big man: 'These people here are scammers. The barman here wants five thousand baht for a little guitar which he claims we broke. It's a scam.'

The big, angry looking man with the malicious grin, looked at each one of the three Thai men. They looked rough, but he looked a lot bigger and rougher. He picked up the little handmade guitar from the table and looked it over. A wooden panel had fallen off. 'This guitar?' the big man said. 'Is this the guitar that is causing the problem?'

The Thai barman said nervously: 'It is handmade and very expensive. It must be repaired by special person.'

Big man: 'Five thousand baht to repair this piece of shit?' He waved it about for a moment, and then smashed it against the table, shattering it and just leaving the wooden handle in his hand. He eyeballed the Thai who had spoken, and then grabbed him by the shoulder before thrusting the sharp edged wood toward the Thai man's neck. 'And how about your fucking funeral? Do we pay for that as well?'

One of the Thai men took out his mobile phone, but Jack clocked it straight away. 'Put that phone away! There's no need to call for any reinforcements. You've been found out and let that be the end of it.'

Big man, waving the dangerous piece of guitar at the Thai men: 'I'll tell you what. Seeing as you three men are behaving like shitheads, I think you owe us all a drink. Go get beers for all the lads, on the house, of course.'

Amazingly, the three Thai men moved towards the bar. Jack stopped them. 'No, we are leaving.' Jack looked at the big man who had saved them. 'Thanks for your help, but we better leave now.'

Kenny nodded. These Thais don't give in easily. Three against two had turned into three against six, but they could call a score of reinforcements given the chance. Time to depart.

Jack and Kenny made for the door and gestured for the others to follow. Get out of there, fast. Quit while you're ahead. All six of the Liverpool men left the bar and began walking towards Beach Road. The big man was the last to leave the bar. Before his exit, he eyeballed the three Thai men. He made a cutthroat gesture with his hand as he said, 'If I hear from you again…'

The six men headed towards Beach Road. Jack was hoping they could lose any trace of themselves and blend in with the other farangs once they got in the busy bars. He and Kenny were still reeling from the ordeal. They had heard of scams in Thailand, but were not prepared for that one. Pattaya may be generally a safe place, probably safer than most other tourist places, but it's still wise to be on your guard.

Jack, to the big man who had got them out of the shit: 'Thanks, mate. I really appreciate that.' He offered the big man his hand.

Big man, shaking Jack's hand: 'I'll do anything for my friend's.'

Kenny, also shaking his hand: 'I didn't catch your name. I'm Kenny and this is Jack.'

Big man, with a friendly, fatherly smile: 'My name is Billy.'

LIZZY BALE

The beach was beautiful. The water was blue and shimmering. The sand was a soft, powdery white. And there was soft, romantic music in the air.

Lizzy looked around the beach. It was deserted except for a lone figure approaching. Lizzy knew who it was. It was her angel, her stallion, the man of her dreams. She ran towards him, her twenty three stone body surprisingly nimble. And as she got closer to her dark, Gambian lover she noticed he had no pants on. He wore a white summery shirt which contrasted beautifully with his black skin. And his chopper….it was big and bold and waving about in the warm sunshine.

Lizzy's man opened his arms as he embraced her, his body

falling to the ground as her twenty three stone body crashed into him. And the two of them were on the sand, rolling about in the waves. She hugged and kissed him sloppily, and then grabbed his mighty willy in her hand. 'My darling,' she said to her Gambian lover. 'You are a real man. Not like my husband. He's inadequate.'

'Lizzy, is everything alright?'

Lizzy awoke in a strange bed. It was dark and then a dim light was switched on. Where was she? She turned to see her husband's wimpy face. 'Oh...' she said. 'I'm here.'

George Bale, suspicious of his wife's dream: 'You said I'm inadequate, Lizzy.'

Lizzy: 'What?'

George: 'You were dreaming. And you said my husband is inadequate.'

Lizzy: 'Did I?'

George: 'Yes you did. What did you mean by that?'

Lizzy, sitting up in bed: 'Oh, don't make anything of it. We all say stupid things in dreams.'

George: 'But it seemed like a very...'

Lizzy, snapping: 'Oh, for fuck's sake, don't make anything of it. It was just a fucking dream, wasn't it. You have enough stupid dreams. Now go and make yourself useful and put the kettle on. I want a pot of tea.'

George, who was half the bodyweight of Lisa, did as he was told. Lizzy continued to lay back in bed, thinking what a wonderful dream that was. That dream was in Gambia, and here she was in Thailand.

Carol was right, Lizzy decided. This place is shit.

Later that afternoon George and Jeff were at the bar whilst the wives were lounging around the swimming pool again.

George: 'I can't believe what I heard coming out of her mouth. She said I'm inadequate.'

Jeff, spitting out his beer: 'What? Fucking inadequate? What kind of word is that?'

George: 'She was dreaming and she said, my husband is inadequate.'

Jeff: 'Big word for Lizzy, that, isn't it? I'd have thought she'd have said something simple like you've got a little dick.'

George, grimacing: 'Well, whatever the fuck, I don't care anymore.' He grinned. 'Besides, we've found something far better.'

Jeff: 'Damn right. I reckon we pay another visit to Soi 6 today.'

George, shaking his head: 'She'd get suspicious and it would be more than my life's worth. Best leave it another couple of days.'

Jeff nodded. 'Yes, and I have my house on the line, as well.'

George: 'Your house on the line. You say that as if…'

Jeff: 'As if what?'

George: 'As if Carol is already threatening to divorce you.'

Jeff, nodding: 'I know what she's after. She's after my house. If she gets her hands on it she'll sell it and probably spend the lot shagging gigolos in Turkey or Gambia or wherever. I just don't trust her anymore.'

George; 'Do you really think that's what they get up to on these holidays to those places, then?'

Jeff, losing patience with his mate: 'Awww, don't be so naive, George. I trusted them at first but when they're going on these girls' holidays all the time, it's obvious what they're up to. I can see it in the bedroom. Carol's just not as excited as before. She used to be hot, but now she just lays back, that's if she can be bothered at all. I reckon she had too many big Gambian cocks. I'm not fucking stupid, George.'

George, pondering: 'Well, that's what they say, isn't it? Once you've had black you'll never go back. I overheard Lizzy saying that once. I thought it was a joke.'

Jeff, his mood becoming more grumpy: 'I'll tell you what, George. Why don't we drink these beers and head down to Soi 6 again? I'm past caring and I just fancy another shag.'

George thought for a moment, then downed his beer, grinning. 'Why the hell not.'

NING

It was now high season and they were all coming out to Thailand. From UK, Germany, Italy, the farangs were finishing their day jobs and heading out to Pattaya for a bit of sun, sea, sand and sex. And so Ning was busy. She now had no less than seven sponsors on the go. And at least four of them were coming to Pattaya during the high season. The other three were easy, coming in the low season where they were unlikely to clash with their rivals. It was the four that were here that she had to go ducking and diving for. And, of course, all seven of them, all seven who were sending her various amounts of money, thought they were the only one. Three were easy. It was these assholes who were here in the high season who were the problem.

So Lee and Ning were sitting across the table from each other at a Beach Road cafe. Lee, who worked hard on a building site all year and relished his time in Thailand with Ning, gazed into the serene, beautiful face of his love.

Ning was glancing at the menu. She liked fish, but had a trick which she thought worked. Instead of ordering the most expensive items on the menu like some of the girls did, she chose the reasonably priced ones. It worked, because it built trust in the men. It made her look less like a gold digger.

Lee: 'I'm so glad I met you again, Ning. I love being here with you.'

Ning, smiling: 'I love being with you, too, Lee.'

Ning was getting more texts on her mobile phone but she ignored them. Thing about Lee, he was a more generous sponsor than the Italian or the German, so he took priority. Another farang would arrive soon so it would be extra awkward.

It was a busy road outside the cafe and there were plenty of people going by. And then, to her horror, Ning, noticed a familiar face. It was Tomas the German. He was walking along the pavement and hadn't noticed her yet. He stopped and glanced at the menu board outside. Ning froze. She hid her face in the menu. When she finally looked up, she saw from the corner of her eye that Tomas had passed. Oh, my.....That would have been a disaster. Thankfully, knowing Tomas's shrewdness with money, the restaurant was probably too expensive for him.

Lee: 'The pork steak with fries looks nice.'

Ning, looking up nervously from her menu: 'Yes. I have the fish.'

It was another day of ducking and diving for Ning. This high season was just beginning. And she had to protect herself and her sponsors. There was big money to be made if she played her cards right.

CHAPTER FIVE

AND THEN THERE WERE SIX

Jack, to Kenny: 'I can't believe it. I just can't fucking believe it.'
Kenny: 'I can't believe it, either. But you must admit, Jack, at that moment when we were in the shit, it was good to see them.'
Jack, nodding into his beer: 'Yes. I got to admit, there are times when you need friends. I was so relieved to see them. I just never thought of these clowns as the Cavalry.'

So the six men from Liverpool were having a night out. They hit the familiar haunts of Walking Street, bars and various go-gos. And, like the first night when the five had first arrived last time, it was a good night. It felt fresh and exciting.

The guys had a story to tell, of course, and Jack and Kenny were listening. Joey's escape from gangsters, Vinnie's win on the horses (that's what he told them) and Pete…poor old Pete ending up in a loony bin. And his friend, Billy. What could you make of him? None of them knew him or what he was all about. But they quickly learned he was Pete's mate, and they had met each other in the loony bin. What!?

Kenny, to Joey: 'So how much do you owe the Gibby's by now, Joey?'
Joey, looking around at the other guys, wondering if he could share this with everyone: 'Fuck knows. It started at about 15 grand, then they told me it was 37, then I escaped from the car, and now….fuck, the way that interest goes up…I don't know, but I haven't got it.'
Jack: 'So what happened when you escaped from the car?

Where did you go?'

Joey, looking at the faces of Billy, and Vinnie, still not sure if he could trust some of his own mates: 'I ended up in a farmhouse with this old couple. Couple of old Welsh farmers. And they were great. They looked after me, I stayed with them for about three months, working on the farm. They were great, and they paid me a bit of money and put a roof over my head and food on the table.'

Jack, grinning: 'Fuck, Joey. I just couldn't imagine you living on a farm with an old Welsh couple. You're a city boy through and through.'

Kenny, grinning: 'And working on a farm. What did you do, shovel manure all day?'

Joey: 'It's not as bad as it sounds. I was just glad to be there.' He looked around the crowded bar, thoughtfully for once. 'They frightened the shit out of me when I was trapped in that car. Those Gibbys are bad men and I thought I was done for. I mean, all I knew is that I needed to lie low, out of sight. And that old couple, well, they were great. I mean, crazy as fuck, but they were good to me. Sometimes, you need good people and right then they were a blessing.'

Vinnie: 'Where they church goers?'

Joey: 'What makes you say that?'

Vinnie: 'I've seen you reading the Bible. I mean, that's not the Joey I know.'

Joey looked away, slightly embarrassed: 'Oh, I dunno. I don't want to talk about it. We're here in Pattaya now. Let's get pissed and shag some women.'

'You've got to cut off the head of the snake first,' Billy was telling them all in a bar close to Beach Road. 'Cut off the head of the snake and the rest doesn't know what to do with itself.'

The other five, Jack, Kenny, Joey, Pete and Vinnie, listened in fascination to Billy's analysis of what he would have done if the bar incident had escalated any further. Billy was aiming his attention at Jack and Kenny, who he didn't know well yet and needed to be indoctrinated into the world of Basket Case Billy. They all just stood there blankly and listened and nodded obligingly. Somehow, the others thought, this wasn't a guy you wanted to argue with or get on the wrong side of.

Billy, analysing the encounter with the three Thai men: 'You see, that one who was doing the talking, well, I'd have shoved that guitar handle through his neck. Shoved it right up through his head and into his brain and then twisted it, watching the blood and brains falling out on the floor. And then the other two would have stood there, pooing their pants. All their fighting skills or whatever they did wouldn't mean a thing then. They would have turned and run like little rabbits in a field when they saw a fox.'

The other men nodded, fascinated, not necessarily for the right reasons.

Later, Jack and Kenny would talk. It didn't take much to figure out this Billy guy was a nutter. And while they owed him for his part in the rescue, this guy was going to take a bit of getting used to. Worse, he could really be a nutter. And that could be a danger to all of them.

CAROL AND LIZZY HIT THE TOWN

'It's fucking shit here,' Carol said as they were in a bar in Soi 8. 'Just look at all these dirty old bastards groping the young girls. That's what it's all about here. Fucking playground for dirty old pervs.'

Lizzy: 'I wouldn't be surprised if George and Jeff were behaving like old pervs behind our backs. Them two keep swanning off somewhere. Just where the fuck are they going?'

Carol: 'I'm past caring. I couldn't give a shite what they get up to.'

Lizzy: 'Well there must have been a reason why they wanted us to come here. They said it was winter sun but they could have chosen the Canary islands.'

Carol: 'Ah, fuck them. Next holiday we're going back to Gambia and we're gonna shag ourselves silly to make up for this shite here.'

A Thai girl approached them at the bar. 'Hello,' she said with a nice Thai smile. 'You alone here? You no have husbands?'

Lizzy, grimacing at this petite young Thai with the skimpy clothes: 'What's it to you?'

Thai girl: 'Ahhhh, you couple?'

Lizzy, looking at Carol: 'Couple?'

Thai girl: 'Yes, together.' She pointed at each one of them. 'You are together? Like couple.'

Lizzy looked blankly at Carol. Carol looked blankly at Lizzy. Then Lizzy looked down at the petite young Thai girl with the friendly smile and said, 'What are you trying to say?'

Carol: 'She's asking us are we Lesbians.'

Thai girl, beaming and standing closer to the two big Western women: 'It's okay. It's okay. I do everything for you. I join you. Or we get other girls, yes? I get my friend and we have foursome.'

Lizzy's face turned dark with anger. She glared at the Thai girl who was a fraction of her size. 'You cheeky little bitch! How fucking dare you? I'll fucking snap you in half...'

Carol, abruptly: 'Cool it, Lizzy! She didn't mean any harm.' Carol turned back to the Thai girl and said, 'No, thankyou, we like men.'

Thai girl, looking wounded: 'Ahhhh, men. You like men?'

Lizzy: 'Yes, we like men not fucking dirty young girls...'

Carol, raising her voice: 'Lizzy, cool it!'

Thai girl: 'Well, if you like men we have Ladyboy. He's with another customer for short time but he should be back soon.'

Lizzy was at a dangerous point right now. She was huge and had a bad temper and had once knocked out a man for calling her Big Lizzy. She could make mincemeat out of this petite Thai girl.

Carol, diffusing the situation: 'Look, can we just pay our bill, please, I think this bar is not for us.'

Outside the bar Lizzy was shouting and swearing and fuming.

Carol was used to Lizzy's temper and was about the only person who could calm her when needed.

Carol, walking down the busy Soi with Lizzy: 'I don't think she meant any harm, Liz. It's just their way. They don't know any different.'

Lizzy: 'Fucking cheeky bitch! Lesbos! Fucking lesbos! Is that what they assume you are if you come here?'

Carol: 'Looks that way, doesn't it.'

Lizzy: 'George said this was a good place. Just why did he want to come here so much? If I hear he's doing anything behind my back I'll fucking strangle him!'

Carol: 'Look, Lizzy, calm down. This place is shit and we both know that by now. Let's go and have a quiet drink. There's a bar over there. Looks nice and quiet.'

Lizzy: 'As long as there are no fucking lesbos in there.'

JOEY AND VINNIE

Joey and Vinnie had never really been the closest of friends. Pete was Joey's best mate out of the group, Vinnie just flitted in and out of the group sporadically. But, on this night out, with Jack and Kenny getting bar girls and disappearing, Pete and that nutter Billy going back to the hotel to talk more shite like they'd been doing all night, Joey and Vinnie formed an allegiance and went off together to have a late night drink. A couple of buddies in good spirits and just glad they were here.

So they found a bar in Soi 13. It was a quiet little bar with just a couple of girls serving and no other customers. Just what they needed to round the night off.

'Two beers,' Vinnie said. The barmaid was an older Thai woman and there didn't appear to be any hassles from girls in this little bar. Just what they needed. Neither Vinnie nor Joey had much money and the hassle to buy girls drinks got a bit much in some of the places they'd been to.

Vinnie, sitting at the bar with Joey: 'So what do you make of this place, Joey?'

Joey, who had had too much to drink: 'I dunno. Seems like a nice enough bar.'

Vinnie, rolling his eyes: 'I meant Pattaya, Joey. What do you think of Pattaya?'

Joey, slurring his words: 'It's alright. Got plenty of birds. It's alright.'

Vinnie: 'I dunno, we're not with any now, are we? Yes, it's a good place but only if you can really afford it. I mean, I like the girls here, they're good fun and all that, but having to pay them all the time. And if you get involved with one you're gonna have to support her and her family and all that.'

Joey: 'Sick buffalo.'

Vinnie: 'Sick what?'

Joey: 'Sick buffalo. That's what people say. If you get involved with her she needs money for the sick buffalo in the village where she comes from.'

Vinnie: 'Ah, yes, I get it. Sick buffalo, Mum and Dad, just about everything else that needs money. Well, they needn't bother looking at me for money coz I haven't got any.'

Joey, slurring his words more with each sentence and making Vinnie wonder where he'd got all the beers from: 'What we need is birds who don't want your money. We want birds who you can shag without paying for it.'

The barmaid was listening to Joey's drunken talk. Vinnie looked at her confused expression, wondering if she knew what they were saying.

Vinnie: 'Yes, I'll drink to that. Need a couple of spare slags but this is not the place for it. All as any of them want is money.'

Just then, two women entered the bar. They were middle aged Western women, both obese, one more than the other. They made their way over to the bar.

Carol: 'Two vodka and tonics, please.'

Lizzy: 'Let's get a seat here.' She moved chairs at a table before sitting her enormous weight down.

Carol: 'No, let's sit at the bar. There's enough seats here.'

Vinnie and Joey looked at the two women, who had Birmingham accents. The two men had ideas already.

The bargirl served the vodka and tonics to the two women. Vinnie clocked the blonde woman, who was not really that overweight compared to the other one. He raised his beer to them: 'Good evening, ladies.'

The two women nodded towards him and his friend: 'Hello,' Carol said.

Vinnie didn't waste time. He moved over to Carol. 'Where are you from? Sounds like Birmingham.'

Carol, nodding: 'Yes, that's right. Are you from Liverpool?'

Vinnie: 'Yes, we're from Liverpool.'

Lizzy: 'Fucking scousers. That's the last thing we need.'

Vinnie, alarmed: 'That's not very nice, is it? Not had a good night? Don't tell me: arguments with the husbands.'

Lizzy: 'Fuck the husbands, it's the fucking lesbos here that get on my tits.'

The conversation had turned a bit hostile, and then Vinnie burst out laughing.

Carol: 'What are you laughing at?'

Vinnie: 'Her! What do you think I'm laughing at?'

Lizzy: 'Are you taking the piss? Fucking scouser, I'd better watch me purse with you around.'

Then Joey, who was getting more drunk by the moment, entered the conversation by going up to Lizzy, getting closer than he should and slurring: 'I'll go back with you. I'll go back to your hotel with you. You and me together.'

Carol and Vinnie both burst out laughing.

Carol: 'Fucking hell, your mate doesn't waste time, does he?'

A few moments later Vinnie and Joey were outside having a smoke. Vinnie was convinced he had scored but was worried drunken Joey would fuck it up.

Vinnie: 'Look, she likes you, that big one. I'll take the other one.'

Joey, slurring: 'The other one. She was looking at me, wasn't she?'

Vinnie: 'Naw, she likes me. Her mate likes you.'
Joey: 'She's big. Like a whale. Big.'
Vinnie: 'Well you like big women, don't you? I mean, she's not just a whale, she's a prize specimen. She's Moby Dick.'
Joey: 'Moby Dick… She's a big whale.'
Vinnie: 'So what, Joey? No one's gonna see you with her. I tell you, we've cracked it. I'll shag the blonde one and you can shag Moby Dick.'
Joey, struggling to lift his drunken head: 'Ah, well, I suppose it's a shag, isn't it?'
Vinnie: 'Yes. And the best bit is we won't have to pay for it.'
This last comment seemed to work. Joey smiled and nodded his head. Yes, that was the good bit.

Carol, whispering to Lizzy: 'He likes you, that drunken one.'
Lizzy: 'He's pissed. The other one doesn't seem so bad.'
Carol: 'Well, I'm up for it. I reckon we go back to their hotel.'
Lizzy: 'Haven't you forgotten something. We have husbands waiting for us.'
Carol: 'Fuck, it'll not gonna be all night. We'll just tell them we got lost on the way home.'

It was a running joke amongst the lads that Joey liked big women. For someone tall, lean and very photogenic (his own description of himself) he had a propensity for ending up with big women. He could pull some nice ones, but once the alcohol kicked in, nothing was too obese for Joey. So Vinnie, who felt he would need a harpoon for Big Lizzy, was glad Joey was pissed so it would get the big one off his hands. And Carol, who was not that much overweight, was actually quite a good looking blonde. Well worth a shag, Vinnie thought.

Vinnie: 'Okay, Joey. Are we up for it? We'll ask them which hotel they are staying in and go back with them.'

Vinnie, to Carol: 'Which hotel are you staying in, Ladies?'
Carol looked at Lizzy. They both shrugged.
Vinnie, thinking that didn't go down well: 'Just asking.'

Joey, pawing at Lizzy and slurring: 'Can we come back to your hotel with yer?'
Carol: 'We can't bring anyone back to the hotel.'
Vinnie thought, for the first time, that they could be married and have their husbands waiting for them. Time for Plan B. 'Okay', Vinnie said. 'In that case we would like to invite you to our hotel. What do you reckon?'

Carol and Lizzy looked at each other. Then back at Vinnie. And then Carol, thinking she had nothing to lose on this shit holiday, said, 'Why the hell not?'

JACK

In Pattaya there is a place known as the Coconut Bar. This is not an actual bar. It is the Beach Road area where the freelancers hang out under the Coconut Trees. It is the area where farangs who don't want to pay for expensive bar girls will go. At the Coconut bar there are no bar fines, no lady drinks and the girls charge a lot less, usually for short time. On the downside, there are no STD checks and the girls can be more dodgy and likely to rob you with no bar to lodge any complaint.

And so Jack, who had had too much to drink and had lost the others, was heading back to his hotel at well beyond midnight. He was walking past the Coconut Bar where there was still plenty of activity even at this ungodly hour. Plenty of freelance girls, farangs, groups of Indians looking for a bargain. Jack was getting lots of hellos from the girls but he wasn't up for it tonight. He'd drunk too much and just wanted to get back to the hotel.

'Jack.'

Jack stopped. It was a female voice under one of the coconut trees. He turned to see a familiar face. He looked at her for a while. She smiled at him. And then he looked at her for a while longer. And then he said, 'Minnie.'

'Jack, you came back. You remember me?'

Jesus, is this what she'd come to? Jack thought. Minnie was the girl he was seeing regularly the last time he was in Pattaya. He had met her in a bar then and now she was working freelance on Beach Road. And then Jack considered that there may not be that much difference between a Thai girl working in a bar and one working freelance on the streets. Whatever, she was here now. And yes, he did remember her. He took her to the island of Koh Samet where they spent New Year together and it was all good until he got suspicious of her constant use of the mobile phone.

  Jack, not knowing what to say: 'Minnie…'

  Minnie, standing closer with a hopeful smile on her face: 'Jack.'

  Jack looked her up and down. She looked beautiful, in her dark top and her white skirt. Just like the Minnie he'd met in a bar last year. But he couldn't help feeling sad. He didn't want to see Minnie here. He was realistic enough to know what working girls were all about, but here, on the street, after midnight…looking for a customer. He felt she was so much better than this.

  Jack: 'What are you doing here, Minnie?'

  Minnie: 'I work, Jack. This is…I'm working. I go with you? You nice man.'

  Jack thought for a moment and then said: 'Why not? Come on, Minnie, let's get away from here. Let's go to my hotel.'

CHAPTER SIX

SO THAT'S HIM, IS IT?

Lenny: 'Well, I hope you are enjoying the show this evening. Now let's just take a walk around the bar and see who's here.'

Lenny Pazazz, during his live YouTube show, would take a walk around his bar and talk to some of the customers. They were often Farangs, mostly British and almost all middle aged with bald heads. They were a friendly bunch though, and a lot of them came to this bar because they liked Lenny, liked his community and wanted to meet the guy who they watched on YouTube. It was all harmless fun.

Lenny, putting his mic towards a grinning baldy: 'And where are you from, Sir?

Baldy: 'Rochdale.'

Lenny: 'Rochdale. Good old Lancashire, eh. Eh up, eh up!'

Baldy, cringing: 'Er…yes.'

Lenny: 'And where are you from, Sir?'

Almost Baldy: 'Glasgow.'

Lenny: 'Glasgow. You've come here to escape the cold Scottish winter. Good for you, mate.'

It was all congenial stuff. The guys came to the bar, spent money on drinks and girls and it was all good for the show.

Lenny, thrusting his microphone at someone who actually had a head of ginger hair: 'And here we have a special guest in the bar. Someone who is appearing for an interview on Friday evening. Hello, Michael.'

Michael, holding up his bottle of Heineken: 'Hello, Lenny. It's good to be here.'

Lenny, turning to the camera: 'Michael is opening up a new bar here in Pattaya and he'll be here to tell us a lot more about it on Friday evening. But, just for the benefit of the viewers, would you like to briefly tell us where you're from and what your bar is all about?'

Michael, turning to the camera: 'Hello, viewers. My name is Michael, I live here in Pattaya and I am from the Netherlands. I have owned bars and clubs here in Pattaya for ten years but I'm now opening my new Ladyboy cabaret bar in Soi Chaiyapoon.'

Lenny: 'That's great. And Micheal will be here on Friday's show for a proper interview where he will tell us what it's like to own bars and clubs in Pattaya. And, he'll be bringing some of his lovely Ladyboys along to give us a show.' Lenny laughed his annoying, cheesy laugh. 'Don't miss that one, viewers. That's on Friday at 9pm Thai time and it's gonna be a real blinder of a show.'

Michael raised his beer to the camera and said, 'See you then.'

PETE AND BILLY

Pete's mouth fell open. He was sitting on the edge of the bed in the hotel room he shared with Billy. And he was looking at Billy's laptop. He was watching the Lenny Pazazz show on Youtube. And his mouth fell open at what he saw.

'That's him,' Pete murmured, his eyes transfixed to the screen. 'That's him.'

Billy was on the balcony with a cup of coffee in his hand, looking out at Pattaya town below him. He came back into the hotel room. 'That's who?'

Pete looked away from the screen and Billy could see the alarm in his face. 'That's him,' Pete said. 'That's the Dutchman.'

Billy, his eyes widening: 'The Dutchman? You mean...'

Billy looked at the laptop screen. He could see a bar with some pansy talking to the camera. 'Where is the Dutchman?'

Pete stopped the show and rewound the video. He played it back for Billy to see and they watched the bit with Lenny Pazazz and the Dutchman. Billy looked closely at Michael, the man who had destroyed the life of his friend.

Billy: 'So that's him, is it? That's the cunt right there, is it?'

Pete: 'Yes, that's him. And he's appearing on that show, in that bar, on Friday at 9pm. It's going to be broadcast live on Youtube.'

Billy looked up at the ceiling. A broad smile cracked over his face. He couldn't believe it. It just seemed so perfect. Couldn't have asked for better, he decided. Already a flood of thoughts and ideas were running through his head

Billy: 'So he's gonna be on that show on Friday at 9pm. Live on Youtube, eh? Live on Youtube.' Billy's grin got even wider. 'Where is this bar, then?'

JEFF AND CAROL

Jeff was asleep in the hotel room. It was dark and he was woken by the key in the door. He opened his eyes to see Carol walking in and switching on the light. Jeff glanced at the clock beside the bed. It was 4.35 am.

Jeff: 'What time do you call this? Where the hell have you been?'

Carol, going into the bathroom for a pee: 'I've been out on the town and I've been having fun.'

Jeff: 'Having fun? With who? Lizzy?'

Carol: 'Lizzy is my friend and we've been having fun together.'

Jeff: 'Till half four in the morning? What kind of time is this to be coming in?'

Carol: 'We've been to a Ladyboy show and it was funny and we got talking to lots of ladyboys and it was a laugh.'

Jeff: 'Fucking ladyboys? Since when were you into that sort of thing?'

Carol, coming out of the bathroom and looking down at her sleepy, pathetic husband: 'I've been going out and having fun with my friend just the same way as you have fun with your friend. Okay?'

Jeff grunted and lay back on the bed. Having fun till four thirty in the morning? Ladyboy shows? WTF?

Later that day, Carol and Lizzy were lying on sunbeds beside the hotel pool. Carol had a cheeky grin on her face. Lizzy had a half grin, not entirely satisfied with last night's outcome.

Carol: 'So what happened? I heard you both shaking on the floor and then you got up and stormed into the bathroom.'

Lizzy: 'The drunken bastard fell asleep. Fucking slobbering all over me. I had to go into the bathroom to wipe myself down.'

Carol: 'He's a nice looking fella, that Joey.'

Lizzy: 'Be a lot nicer if he weren't pissed.'

Carol thought that if Joey wasn't pissed he wouldn't have attempted to shag Lizzy in the first place. She grinned to herself.

Carol: 'Well, mine went well. He's alright, that Vinnie. We did our bumping and grinding without a problem. He was rock hard and hungry.' She laughed. 'Who would have thought when we came to this shithole that we'd have ended up shagging two Scousers?'

George and Jeff were having a drink over at the poolside bar. Neither of them were happy.

George: 'Four thirty? Is that what it was? I was asleep.'

Jeff: 'Yes, four fucking thirty when she came waltzing in through the door. Not even bothering an explanation. Then she said something about a Ladyboy bar or something.'

George: 'Yes, that's what Lizzy said. They said they were at a ladyboy show and they got talking to the ladyboys and it was all harmless and…shite.'

Jeff: 'Sounds like they've concocted the same fucking excuse, to me.'

George: 'Well, what are you saying? Do you reckon they've been up to no good?'

Jeff: 'They've been doing something they shouldn't have. I could tell it in Carol's attitude. When she shows that kind of arrogance I know she's got something to hide.' He knocked back his beer and slammed the bottle on the bar. 'Well, two can play at that game. Come on, George. I think it's time we went for another visit to Soi 6.'

George grinned and swigged his beer: 'Now you're talking!'

JACK AND MINNIE

Jack was sad. He hadn't felt so sad in a long time.
Jack had brought Minnie back to his hotel and they had spent the night together. Slept in the bed together. Boom boom together. But it wasn't the fun he was used to.

As morning broke and Minnie lay fast asleep in his bed, he felt sad that it had come to this. Minnie on the streets. A street hooker. He thought he would never see that.

Last year he had met Minnie in a bar and she had won him over, more than the other Thai girls he had met. And she didn't seem as opportunistic as the others. She seemed genuine. Until he got paranoid about her use of the mobile phone and constant texts. But, he thought, maybe that said more about him. He just couldn't trust anyone.

But Minnie waiting on Beach Road, waiting for customers? Jack was quite shocked. He thought she was above all that. He turned to look at her serene face as she slept. Still the same beautiful Minnie. Her looks hadn't changed. So what else had changed? Something in her life must have changed. Or was he naive in thinking that a bar girl was a more stable girl than a Coconut Bar freelancer?

Either way, Jack was sad. And he felt guilty. If he was a more trusting person he would have looked after her. But, then, Lee looked after Ning, didn't he? And she seemed to be shunning his sudden arrival, probably coz she's got other customers on the go.

Jack and Minnie spent the day together. They had a walk along the beach and then had a nice dinner in a beachfront restaurant. It cheered both of them up and Jack liked having her company again. He decided to put behind whatever had caused her to end up as a street freelancer and decided they would see each other again. He wasn't worried about making a big mistake. He was wise enough to this game by now. He just wanted to be with Minnie again.

Jack, sitting across the table from Minnie at a beachfront bar: 'So what have you been doing all year, Minnie?'

Minnie, shrugging, sipping her cola: 'Working. Low season not been good. I need to make money. I have family in Isaan. They very poor.'

Jack looked out to sea. He'd heard all the stories before about poor families and sick buffalos. He swore it wouldn't happen to him the way it had to Lee. But, as he looked across the table to the beautiful face of Minnie, he still couldn't put her in the same category as those devious, gold digging Thai girls he'd heard so much about. There was something more genuine about Minnie and Jack felt that, given the right chance, she would prove to be a fine partner. He'd have to think very carefully about what would happen when he went back to the UK. For now, Jack was with Minnie and it felt so good to be with her again.

VINNIE AND JOEY

The six men were having a drink late afternoon in a bar complex in Soi Buakow. The beer was cheap and the weather was lovely so they could overlook the fact that this inland area of Pattaya is really grim. Plenty of life about, but not exactly a tropical paradise, more of a Third World slum.

Billy: 'Is this still Thailand?'

Kenny: 'I know what you mean. It doesn't exactly feel like an exotic location here.'

Jack: 'I've seen Liverpool council estates that look better than here.'

Pete: 'There's nothing looks as bad as a Liverpool Council Estate. I wouldn't tarnish anywhere with that brush.'

Jack thought how Pete was not the Pete of old. His stay in a loony bin and whatever led him there had clearly done some irreparable damage. The guy didn't even talk the same. He hardly talked at all and when he did, he seemed slower. Like a guy with a low IQ, which Pete certainly wasn't. He was college educated to an extent, and could have made something of his life if his bad habits of booze and borrowing and laziness hadn't got in the way.

As for Pete's mate Billy, well, the rest of the group had by now formed a positive opinion of Billy. They had decided he was positively doolally, crazy, unbalanced, not a full shilling, a few sandwiches short of a picnic. In other words, a liability. They knew to be on their guard with this stranger.

So they were at a bar table and a new round of beers had been ordered and they were all in good spirits. And then Kenny said: 'Come on, then Vinnie. Tell us the details. We wanna know who this Brummy girl was you shagged last night.'

Vinnie beamed. He'd been beaming all day. 'Well, she was alright. I mean, a bit heavy but I kind of like a real woman. And she was a damn good shag. No problems, she was well up for it.'

Jack: 'So where did you shag her?'

Vinnie: 'In the bed back at Joey's room. Fucked like rabbits, we did. Almost broke the bed. Dirty bitch, as well,' Vinnie grinned. 'I like a good dirty woman.'

Kenny: 'And how about you, Joey? You haven't said much about your bird.'

Joey, shrugging: 'I can't remember. I was pissed.'

Vinnie, laughing; 'It was fucking funny. I was shagging hell out of Carol and he was on the floor with the other one and then he...' Vinnie banged the table with laughter, '...he threw up over her! I heard her swearing and running off to the bathroom and he crashed out asleep on the floor. It was a hoot!'

The guys laughed. It sure sounded like Joey.

VINNIE AND JOEY MEET THE GIRLS

A couple of hours later Vinnie and Joey went out together to meet Carol and Lizzy. Vinnie had received a text from Carol and they were to meet at the same bar in Soi 13.

Vinnie ordered two beers for him and Joey. The girls hadn't arrived yet.

Joey, drinking his beer: 'I can't remember a fucking thing about last night. How long did we stay out last night? I haven't got a clue what she looked like. Can't even remember being here in this bar.'

Vinnie, still beaming from the result last night: 'Awwww, don't worry. You enjoyed yourself last night. Just don't throw up again this time.'

A couple of minutes later Vinnie could see Carol and Lizzy walking toward the bar. 'Here they are,' Vinnie said, turning his back to the bar to greet them. As the two women walked into the bar Vinnie did not notice the look of shock horror on Joey's face.

Carol, beaming as she approached Vinnie: 'Hiya, love. How are yer?' She gave Vinnie a sloppy kiss and Vinnie hugged her tightly.

Lizzy approached Joey, who stood with his mouth open. She grinned at him and then, noticing his look of alarm, stood back. 'What's the matter with you?' she said.

Joey turned to Vinnie. He looked at Vinnie, who was still grinning, then he looked at Carol, who was grinning, and then he looked back at the twenty three stone monster. And she wasn't grinning. And neither was Joey.

They all fell silent. And then Joey said, 'I'm going outside for a smoke.'

Joey went out in silence and lit up a cigarette. A minute later Vinnie went to join him.

Vinnie: 'What's the matter with you?'

Joey, looking blankly at the street: 'Are you taking the piss?'

Vinnie, his grin dropping: 'What? Why? What's the problem?'

Joey, sounding more angry: 'Are you taking the fucking piss out of me?'

Vinnie, assessing the situation: 'Joey, you were with her last night. You shagged her last night. No, I am not taking the piss.'

Joey: 'Fuckoff! No fucking way did I touch that fucking beast!'

Vinnie, nodding: 'You did, Joey. You were pissed, mind, but you shagged her on the floor of the hotel room. And I shagged the blonde one in the bed.'

You see, some guys can handle their drink more than others. Some guys get drunk and fall asleep, some guys get drunk and cause trouble, some guys get drunk and throw up and some guys get drunk and, no matter how they behave or what happens, they can't remember a thing the next day. Of these scenarios, the only one not typical of Joey is the first one. He rarely falls asleep getting drunk.

Joey, throwing his cigarette on the floor and angrily stubbing it out with his foot: 'I'm going. I'm fucking getting out of here.'

Joey walked away. He didn't even go back to the bar to finish his beer. He just turned and went. Vinnie called after him, but it was not good.

Vinnie walked back into the bar to see Carol and her monster friend standing there, looking puzzled. 'What's the matter with him?' Carol said.

Vinnie shrugged: 'I think he's on his period.'

GEORGE AND JEFF

'Ohhh, you big man! You big man!'

George was having the time of his life. He was loving Soi 6, and the hot girls there.

For those who have never come across this gem of Pattaya, Soi 6 is a narrow road at the other end of Pattaya to the well known Walking Street. Walk along Beach Road and keep walking and, just when you think all the nightlife and bars and naughty stuff is over, up pops Soi 6. A narrow street full of girly bars with lashing of sexy Thai girls in skimpy clothes, usually a uniform to promote their bar, and an irresistible policy for a man on the prowl. Go in and have a drink, be approached by a sexy girl and before you know it it's upstairs for a bit of short time rumpy pumpy. Leave with a big grin on your face.

George, putting his pants back on in an upstairs short time room: 'That was magic. Here's a nice tip.'

Thai girl, counting the money, her eyes widening: 'Ohhhh, thankyou, you nice man.' She hugged and kissed him. 'You come back visit me again.'

George loved these Thai girls. Absolutely loved them. This slender cutie was twenty five years old and he was having more fun with her in an hour than he'd ever had shagging his twenty three stone wife. George grinned wide before staggering down the stairs to the bar. He ordered another drink while he waited for Jeff to come down. Five minutes later, Jeff came down the stairs. He also had a broad grin. George and Jeff gave each other a high five. They'd never had so much fun in years. What a great choice they'd made coming to Pattaya.

A short while later, George and Jeff were sitting in a Beach Road bar having a cold beer and watching the sun go down over the sea.

Jeff: 'Ahhhh, you can't beat this place, can you?'

George, nodding: 'You're not wrong there. Why did it take us so long to come here?'

Jeff: 'God knows. I heard about Pattaya long ago, but Carol wouldn't entertain the idea.'

George: 'I wonder why….'

Jeff, grinning: 'Something to do with all these sexy young girls after the dirty old men.'

George, grinning: 'You know, I still love her.'

Jeff: 'What? Who?'

George: 'Lizzy. I still love her. I mean, in spite of what anyone says. I know she's big and ugly, but we've been together so long I couldn't imagine living without her. She's been my rock over the years.'

Jeff, hearing this before: 'Well, that's up to you, George. I must admit, I don't think I'd have been with Carol so long if it wasn't for the house.'

George: 'Really?'

Jeff: 'She's too aggressive. Too much swearing. Too much attitude. Drives me nuts. I've often thought she's just looking for an excuse for me to slip up so she can divorce me and take that house. My house, the one that I've bought and worked so hard for. She wouldn't hesitate to rob me of that in a divorce court. Ahhhh, she can be a right bitch when she wants to be.'

LIZZY

Lizzy was in the bathroom, looking at her reflection. She didn't like what she saw. Never had done. She looked at this big, six foot, obese, dragon-like image and felt like smashing the mirror.

What had happened with that Scouser, the one who she had been shagging the night before? Did he deliberately throw up on her? And tonight, why did he run off? It was obvious, he'd sobered up and realised she was a beast. Fucking bastard. I'll twat him if I see him again, she thought.

Lizzy was hurt. She knew she was fat and ugly. She always had been. Even as a child she was a monster, teased by the boys and feared by the girls. Big Lizzy, they had called her at school. Even today she hated being called that. A few years back she had knocked a man out in a pub for calling her Big Lizzy. It gained her a reputation and it led to her working as a bouncer in the local clubs. That's where she met George. He was little and puny and couldn't pull a bird. But he liked Lizzy, for whatever reason a puny little man would be attracted to a big, powerful monster of a woman twice his bodyweight. It takes all kinds. It wasn't long before they got married and had been with each other for over twenty years. Not a romance made in Heaven but it seemed to work well enough.

Lizzy heard a noise. It was the door opening. George was back at the hotel. Oh, well, she thought, at least she had a husband. Even though he was a useless little dick.

George came into the hotel humming to himself. 'George, where have you been?'

George, opening the fridge and grabbing a beer: 'Hello, my sweet. I've been around the town with Jeff. Just having a lads day out together.'

Lizzy: 'Where exactly?'

George, switching the TV on and lying back on the bed: 'Oh, just around. Few bars, that sort of thing. Nothing much.'

Nothing much, eh? Lizzy thought. Then why did he appear so cheerful? Something told her he'd had a better day than she had.

CAROL AND VINNIE

Carol and Vinnie snuggled up in bed with each other. They were both pleased as punch they had met each other.

Carol, playing with Vinnie's dick: 'Who would have thought, eh? Who would have thought?'

Vinnie, grinning: 'Who'd have thought what?'

Carol: 'That I'd come all this way to Thailand and ended up in bed with a Scouser!'

Vinnie: 'A nice Scouser. A nice Scouser and a nice Brummie.'

Carol: 'Ahhhhh, you're so nice. A pity about that mate of yours.'

Vinnie: 'Well, he's an awkward one, he is. I wouldn't worry about him.'

Carol: 'I don't blame him for walking off on Lizzy. I mean, he was so pissed when he went with her that it must have been a shock when he saw her again.'

Vinnie: 'She's big, isn't she? I mean, Joey's been with some big women but she's a real whale. Moby Dick,' he laughed.

Carol, frowning: 'Eh, don't say that to her if you see her again. I mean, the worst thing you can ever call her is Big Lizzy. She hates that. She's really touchy about her size.'

Vinnie: 'Big Lizzy? I'd say that's one of the kinder things you can call her.'

Carol, looking serious: 'No, don't ever, ever call her that. I once saw her knock out a man for calling her that.'

Vinnie, alarmed: 'Okay, I'd better remember that.'

Carol: 'I felt sorry for your mate, though. I mean, he's a good looking guy. I bet he could pull loads of birds.'

Vinnie, his smile dropping: 'Joey? Oh, he does, I suppose. Why, do you fancy him?'

Carol: 'No, don't be silly. He's nice, but not as nice as you.'

Somehow Vinnie didn't believe her. He had an idea she had the hots for Joey. That's not good, he decided.

Carol, climbing on top of Vinnie for another round of hot, steamy sex: 'Typical Scouser, aren't you, Vinnie?'

Vinnie: 'What makes you say that?'

Carol, laughing: 'You've stolen my heart?'

They both laughed as they bumped and grinded a bit more, with Carol forgetting she had a husband and Vinnie thinking he may have competition from Joey.

CHAPTER SEVEN

A STRANGE FRIENDSHIP

Pete had formed a close friendship with Billy. He wasn't the kind of friend Pete would normally make. In fact, if Pete was of sound mind he would not only have thought twice, but run a mile. Billy was clearly not the friend Pete would have made if he was of sound mind. Unfortunately, since his breakdown or whatever it was, Pete was not of sound mind. After being beaten and disowned by his family he had gone off the rails and ended up in that loony bin place. And, at a time when no one else wanted to befriend him, Billy was the one who offered him friendship. Someone to talk to. Most importantly, someone on his side.

And so they had ended up, here, in Pattaya, the trip paid for by Billy who had inherited a house from his Aunt. And while Billy was clearly unbalanced it didn't matter too much to Pete. He had ended up in that loony bin place, so he wasn't one to judge others. In truth, Pete didn't care about anything anymore.

Pete's bad fortune had just snowballed. The last year had been the worst year of his life. What a way to enter your thirties. He had once been a promising young man, intelligent, from one of the more stable Liverpool families. Mum and Dad both had good jobs, and then they had divorced and his Dad went to live in Los Angeles. Pete had visited L.A., a real thrill for him as a teenager. And he felt ambitious then. He planned to join his Dad when he was old enough. So he went to University and his Mother had such high hopes for him. He was not like other local Liverpool lads he had grown up with. Pete was intelligent, read a lot of books, excelled at Mathematics and Science. He was a bright lad who could have done good for himself. Except, intelligence and discipline are not the same thing. He eventually got bored with University, dropped out and started making friends with the local wasters in his Liverpool area of Huyton. He tried a number of unskilled, tedious jobs, but left or got fired simply because he didn't want to work. Pete was lazy. Then, in his twenties, he started borrowing from people. It became a habit. He became a notorious borrower, an Owlarse, as they say in Liverpool. He lost any decent friends he had and formed a close bond with Joey, another notorious Owlarse. And then, out of work, he started claiming sickness benefit. There was nothing wrong with him, but it was well known you got more money from the Social Security system if you claim Sickness Benefit. So he had a doctor prescribe him with depression and Alcohol Dependency, and at least it brought him regular money and meant there was no pressure to work anymore. So, in his twenties, Pete became a dosser, as it is known. Someone who doesn't want to work and is content to claim benefits. But money was tight and Pete, like Joey, needed those nights out and a social life. So he borrowed and borrowed, and gambled the money he had borrowed, and soon got a bad reputation. And his luck ran out when he borrowed off the wrong crowd and got badly beaten up for not paying the money back. But it didn't cure him. By then, it had become a way of life.

And then came Thailand, Pattaya, last year. Pete had seen Jack and Kenny booking that flight for a brand new adventure, and he and Joey didn't want to be left out. So Joey, already massively in debt, borrowed from loan sharks. And Pete did something no son should ever, ever do. He stole his Mother's bank card. Yes, he kidded himself that it was alright, she had thousands of pounds in there and she wouldn't miss it. She had other bank cards. He'd pay her back one day, when he had the money, whenever he had a lottery win or whatever. Pete knew her pin number because he helped her shop quite often. And he took the card to Thailand and blew his Mother's savings on a lads holiday in Pattaya. It was only when his Mother's credit card direct debit bill was rejected that she realised her card had gone missing. A visit to the bank revealed the money had been spent in Thailand.

So Pete, on his return home, was beaten up by his own brother. And the rest of the family gave him a kicking, too. Hospitalised him. And it didn't end there. Soon after his release, still with broken bones, Pete strayed into the wrong pub in Liverpool and ran into a guy he had owed money to for a long time. Pete got beat up again. More broken bones. Back in hospital. And then he had his breakdown.

Pete was sectioned and ended up in a Psychiatric Ward. And that's where he met Billy. And Billy, his now closest friend, was the only one Pete had confided in about what really happened when he had been kidnapped in Pattaya. Pete hadn't told the others, Jack, Kenny, and Joey, about how he was drugged and tied up and violated by Ladyboys, all for the warped satisfaction of Sado Masochistic freaks for their sordid entertainment. Vinnie knew about it, because he was employed at that shady club, given plenty of ganja to keep him happy. But it was Billy who Pete gave all the lurid details to. Pete was totally honest to Billy about how he was buggered by a Ladyboy, and then kidnapped and tied up and violated and humiliated. And that Dutchman, that bastard Michael, was the one filming it all for his sick videos. Dutch Michael was the one who had instigated it all. Dutch Micheal was responsible for Pete, a thirty year old man, being sexually abused in the most humiliating circumstances. And if there was one person Pete was going to hold responsible for his breakdown, it was Dutch Michael. All he knew is that he wanted to see that Dutch cunt suffer as he himself had suffered during the kidnap ordeal.

And Billy was the man who was going to make that happen.

Billy: 'Look at this shop, here, Pete. Wow, they've got a right grand collection here.'

Pete and Billy stopped outside a weapons store on Second Road. They gazed in the window at the arsenal of knives, guns, machetes. All the equipment needed to do a lot of damage to people.

Billy: 'Let's go inside.'

'Sawadika,' said the man behind the counter. 'How are you, Gentlemen?'

Billy and Pete both grinned at him as they looked around the place. It was a well established store, with nice displays of both costumes and weapons. Billy looked at the knives first.

'Show me the knives,' he said to the Thai man.

The Thai man opened up the glass case and took out several long knives and began to give them a detailed description. He clearly knew his stuff. Billy was impressed.

Thai man: 'Where you from, Sir?'

Billy, eyeing a machete: 'England.'

Thai man: 'You like this one, Sir? This is traditional Thailand machete, used many thousands of years ago to fight invaders.'

Billy, picking up the machete, and handling it lovingly: 'Awwwww, it's a lovely piece of kit.'

Thai man: 'Yes, very nice, Sir. And look at the design on handle. Traditional Thailand design. Very nice.'

Billy, touching the steel and looking carefully at the sharp blade: 'How much?'

Thai man: 'Four thousand, five hundred baht for that one, Sir.'

Billy: 'Let's see a few knives.'

The Thai man showed him an array of impressive knives. But it was the machete that Billy liked best. He picked up the machete in his big, strong right hand and made a cutting movement through the air. Then he made another, faster movement. And then another. Yes, he thought. This was the one. This was the blade that would make him famous.

Billy: 'I'll take this one.' He also chose several, smaller knives and two black, silk robes.. He grinned at Pete and said, 'We sure are gonna look the part'.

Thai man: 'If you leave a forwarding address we can mail them to your own country.'

Billy, lovingly caressing the lethal blade of the machete: 'Won't be necessary.'

JACK, KENNY, JOEY AND VINNIE

The problem with introducing a Thai girlfriend to your mates is that they can sometimes give her the strangest look. The look of, 'don't I know you from somewhere'. Or worse, 'have I had you before'. This was the case when Jack and Minnie were at a Beach Road bar and in comes Kenny, Joey and Vinnie. They all sat down together and Jack did the introductions.

Kenny, to Minnie: 'Have I seen you before?'

Minnie, shaking her head: 'No. I no see you before.'

Joey: 'It's, er, Minnie. Good to meet you.'

Vinnie, to Minnie: 'You look familiar.'

Jack: 'Oh, for fuck's sake, none of you have seen her before. I'm sure you're only trying to wind me up.'

Jack ordered a round of drinks for everyone. It was another blazing hot day and a Beach Road bar was the place to be. The guys quickly got used to Minnie and Minnie got used to them. It was a good atmosphere between all.

Kenny: 'So what happened to your Brummy bird then, Joey?'

Joey, his head sinking to the table: 'Don't ask. Just don't fucking ask.'

Jack: 'Did you do the business?'

Joey, looking grumpy: 'I just said, don't fucking ask.'

They all nodded. Then Vinnie, beaming, said, 'I did. She loves me.'

They all looked at each other and shrugged. Well, Vinnie wasn't able to splash out on expensive Thai girls so a Brummie tourist was ideal. He'd landed on his feet.

Joey, spitting his beer out: 'Just how the fuck did I end up with Moby Dick?'

They all looked knowingly at each other, and laughed.

Jack: 'Oh, it's all coming out now. So she was a big whale, was she?'

Kenny: 'Don't tell me, Joey. You were pissed and didn't know what you were doing.'

Same old Joey, they all thought. For a guy who liked to boast about being tall, lean and photogenic, he had a propensity to end up with the fat ones. And then claim it was coz he was pissed and didn't know what he was doing.

BASKET CASE BILLY

Billy loved his new toy. He stood in the centre of the hotel room and practised swinging it through the air.

Billy: 'Whoosh. Whoosh. Whoooooooosh.'

The machete was perfect. The knives were a backup, but it was the machete that was the real star. So shiny and stylish and sharp, he practised swinging it over and over again.

'Whooooosh. Whooooosh. Whooooooshhhhh.'

Pete sat on the balcony drinking a beer and gazing out to Pattaya town. He wondered what he was getting into. Could be something really bad. Dangerous. Total disaster. But, you know what? Pete didn't care. He didn't care about anything anymore. Whatever Billy had planned it was his business. Pete would just let him get on with it. And if they both ended up in one of those awful Thai prisons, well, it couldn't be any worse than the loony bin where he'd met Billy. Pete would just hang himself, put an end to it all.

Billy held up the machete and gazed at his reflection in the wall mirror. He looked impressive. When he put on the black silk robe and started waving that machete he would make them all wet their pants. He grinned, thinking of the looks of terror he would get.

'Whoooosh. Whooooshhhh.'

Billy knew what people called him back home. Basket Case Billy. He'd heard it many times, first as a joke and then, when he realised it was an insult, he'd clobbered a few people for it. It was clear from an early age that Billy was not going to settle into conventional working life. His few early jobs had ended with him assaulting his employers. He was regarded as unemployable. He'd then tried several businesses, market stalls, but he frightened the customers off. So Billy slipped into crime. He'd done time for violence and robbery. In fact, at forty two years old, most of his adult life had been spent behind bars. And he carried with him a fearsome reputation. You don't mess with this guy. From his scary, big frame and muscular physique to his love of weapons, this was a guy who was ready at a moment's notice to do serious violence. Some were amazed he hadn't yet committed murder. Others believed he had but had gotten away with it. Maybe even murdered the witnesses, or left them too scared to speak. His name had been linked to murders in the Liverpool underworld but nothing had ever been proven.

So now Billy was here, Thailand, a place he'd heard of but never been before. And, as he waved his beloved machete about in the air, he believed he had a purpose. A cause. That cause was to wreak vengeance on the man who had destroyed his friend's inner soul. Left Pete, a fine young man from Liverpool, into a nervous wreck. Michael, the evil Dutchman and his army of Ladyboys, who had buggered the soul from Billy's friend. No one does that to a friend of Billy's. No one.

And as Billy waved his machete about he thought that things couldn't be more perfect. A YouTube show, live on air, being broadcast to thousands across the world. A show to remember. A show that would make Billy famous. Billy, the man who beheaded the evil Dutchman live on air. A shocking moment of violence that would put him in the halls of fame alongside the greats of West, Sutcliffe and Manson. Billy smiled. What a mouth watering prospect. Except, it was better than that. All those killers had been perceived as villains, whereas Billy was going to be a hero. Billy and Pete, the heroes who had delivered true justice to an evil sex offender live on air. Now that's something you don't see everyday.

CAROL AND JEFF

Jeff was sitting up in bed as Carol walked through the door. He glanced at the electric clock beside the bed. Four twenty three am.

Carol: 'You still awake?'

Jeff: 'What time do you call this?'

Carol, heading for the bathroom: 'Oh, don't give me any of that. Go back to sleep.'

Jeff was angry. Waltzing in here in the early hours, not even giving an explanation. Just who does she think she is? And who does she think her husband is? Some fucking dickhead?

Jeff: 'Where have you been exactly, Carol?'

Carol came out of the bathroom and began getting undressed. 'I've been out with my friend Lizzy and we've had a good night. We're on holiday, remember?'

Jeff: 'Good night, eh? Except this is fucking morning now.'

Carol, not taking any grief from old fuckface: 'Oh, shut it. What are you trying to say? Just go back to sleep.'

Jeff: 'And how do I know what you've up to, then? You could have met some fucking gigolo for all I know.'

Carol, hesitating before getting into bed: 'Gigolo? Pattaya is too shite to have gigolos. They have them in other countries.'

Jeff: 'What? Like Gambia and Turkey, you mean?'

Carol, turning away from Jeff as her head touched the pillow: 'Ohhhh, give it a rest, will yer? You're sounding like a right fucking moaner. Just turn the light off and go to sleep.'

Jeff turned the light off, but he didn't go to sleep. He was angry. This bitch was his wife and she was taking the piss out of him one way or the other. And he knew she had him by the balls. Their marriage had become loveless, more sarcastic. And he no longer trusted her. And now that he'd seen what Thailand had to offer he didn't care too much for Carol any more. It was his house that he cared for. The house that he'd worked his bollocks off for over the years. Jeff's house that he had bought. He knew this bitch would take it from him given the chance. And anything else she could lay her hands on. And what would she spend all the divorce money on? The answer probably lay in Gambia or Turkey.

NING AND HER SPONSORS

Ning was lying in bed in Marco's hotel. Marco was sitting on the balcony. It was morning and the Italian man liked to drink coffee while watching the sunrise.

Ning sat up in bed and switched on her mobile phone. A minute later there were all the overnight texts coming in. Tomas had been phoning her. Lee had been texting her. More messages from other sponsors and a few friends. She was a busy girl and struggled to keep up with her popularity. But the peak season, when the guys were more likely to come to Pattaya, was a particular problem. The problem was seeing them often enough to keep them sweet whilst not letting them know about each other. It was a close one the other day when she was sitting in that cafe with Lee and then Tomas walked past. That would have been a disaster. You don't just lose one sponsor when that happens. You lose two.

'Bongiorno,' Marco said, beaming as he walked back into the bedroom to refill his coffee cup. 'And how are you, my princess?'

Ning, rubbing her eyes and putting her phone beneath the covers: 'Good morning, Marco, my love.'

Marco made two cups of coffee for him and his lady. He brought the coffee to the bedside and kissed her on the forehead. He liked being romantic, and knew that his lady just loved it.

Marco: 'Today, we stay together. Let's go to the beach and lie on a sunbed and then I take you to a nice restaurant. One with a view overlooking the sea.'

What girl could resist this? It sounded so romantic, except Tomas and Lee had been hovering around the beach area during their stay and if she accepted Marco's invitation then it was only a matter of time before disaster occurred.

Ning, hugging Marco: 'I thought we'd do something different, today. How about Jomtien beach? It's much nicer than Pattaya. And there's some nice restaurants in Pratumnak. I can show you some nice ones you've never been to.'

Ning was correct. Jomtien beach was nicer than Pattaya and also had some nice restaurants nearby. And she was less likely to bump into the other mugs.

Marco, grinning: 'For you, my dear, anything.'

Ning hugged Marco tightly. Anything, did he say? That wasn't exactly true because other sponsors were far more generous than this ageing Italian lothario. He gave her more money than Tomas but not as much as Lee. It was the last one that she had to protect. He who gives the most money wins the girl. That's business.

JACK, KENNY AND LEE

Jack and Kenny rarely had arguments between them, but Kenny voiced his opinion when Jack started bringing Minnie along with him on their nights out. 'What the fuck are you bringing a bird with you for? It's supposed to be a lads night out, isn't it?'

Yes, it was a lads night out. And Jack, Kenny and Lee, who had become a good mate who wasn't a problem and always had money, were a good little group to be out with. But Jack had since met Minnie again, and, whether it was guilt for dumping her last time or pity that he found her on the streets once again, he wanted to be with her. He liked Minnie, refused to accept she was a gold digger like the other girls were and just wanted to be with her. But he didn't want to desert his mates like he had last time.

They were in a bar together, Jack, Kenny, Lee and Joey. And, yes, Jack had brought Minnie with him.

Jack, to Kenny: 'Look, Kenny, I know what you're thinking. Coz I'd think the same. But, come on, this is Minnie. She's a good girl. You've all met her and gotten used to her by now. If me and her end up together then she's gonna be around all the time, isn't she?'

Kenny: 'I don't dislike the girl, I just think if we are gonna have a lads night then it should just be the lads. I mean, I wouldn't bring a girl to a lads night out.'

Jack: 'Yes, but you must admit, she's different. I mean, you've talked to her enough. She's not like the other girls. She's more like, well, one of the lads. You can have a laugh with her. She speaks good English. She can take a joke.'

Joey, grinning: 'One of the lads? She's not hiding something down there, is she?'

Jack, unflinching: 'Oh that's hilarious, Joey. I'm rolling about in my chair over that one.'

Joey, grimacing: 'Okay, no need to be sarky.'

Jack, to Kenny: 'Minnie's down to Earth. Give her a chance. You'll get to like her after a while. And remember, I'm not expecting anyone else to pay for her. I'll be buying the drinks for her so she's not gonna cost you anything.'

Minnie had heard most of the talk about her. She liked that Jack didn't keep any secrets from her. She understood what his friends were thinking. But no more was said of it. They'd just have to get used to her.

It didn't take long before the other lads got used to Minnie. She had such a winsome, harmless personality and didn't intrude on their behaviour. Kenny continued barfining girls from the bars, Lee continued flitting back and forth between his new group of friends and his girlfriend Ning, Joey continued sponging drinks off the rest of the group, Vinnie seemed preoccupied with this Brummy woman he was shagging and Pete and Billy didn't go out too much with the rest of the group. The others had their concerns about Billy and wanted to distance themselves from him. But their concerns came to a head when they met him the following night in a bar in Soi Diana.

It was the area where Kenny, Joey and Pete had had some serious shit last Christmas.

I DON'T HOLD YOUR HAND BUT I HAVE GOT YOUR BACK

Jack wasn't present last time when the lads had had trouble at the bar in LK Metro. If he was aware of where they were going that night he would have had something to say.

Things were going okay early on in the evening. The night had begun in a quiet bar in Soi Diana and it was a good opportunity for the rest of the boys to get to know Billy.

There were five of them present in the bar, Jack, Kenny, Joey, Pete and Billy. Minnie was there, also, keeping a low profile. And Billy was talking. This guy could talk, for sure. He regaled them all with his stories of Liverpool and gangsters and violence and other gibberish. Some of the lads seemed interested, others thought it a yawn, heard it all before sort of thing. Jack wasn't impressed. This was Thailand, and he hadn't come all this way to hear about Liverpool. He wanted to forget that place for the month he was here.

Billy: 'Looks, lads, I just want to say a big thankyou for what you did for my friend, Pete, last year. Pete's told me all about it.'

Kenny: 'You mean, the Sadomasochism club?'

Billy, nodding: 'That's the one. Pete's told me all the details. And I must say how impressed I was. Absolutely amazing that you guys showed real courage going into that place and rescuing this poor man from a fate worse than death. Now that's what I call true friendship. And if I'd have been there I'd have been fighting alongside you.'

They all looked at each other and had a moment of pride. They rescued Pete because, in spite of all their differences, he was still their mate. And when mates go out or on holiday together, they stick together and are there for each other when they need to be. Nothing corny about that.

Billy: 'True fighting spirit, that's what you lads have. True fighting spirit.' Billy raised his beer bottle and they all clinked bottles. Jack wondered what Billy would look like in a leather thong like the rest of them had to wear. Perhaps he would have enjoyed it.

It was a good atmosphere. They were all getting used to Billy, and he seemed to like them. But they were still learning about him. They'd need to learn about him before they could trust him, especially since he was a guy with such obvious potential for violence. You don't take that lightly.

Billy: 'So what's this other business we need to sort out.' They noticed he included the word 'we'. He was one of them now.

The lads looked at each other, puzzled. Then Kenny said, 'You mean the fight at the bar around the corner from here?'

Billy, nodding and looking at Joey: 'Was it you who got sparked out, Joey?'

Joey, looking embarrassed: 'Yes. Some Yorkshire cunt caught me off guard. No warning. Just…bam.' Joey made a gesture with his fist. 'Knocked me right back over the tables.'

Billy, nodding: 'That's bad. That's very bad.'

Kenny: 'And that fucking Ladyboy, stamping on my head with his stiletto. My head was bleeding to fuck.'

Billy: 'That's terrible. That's fucking terrible.' Then Billy smiled, that dangerous, sinister smile they had now gotten used to. 'Well, we can't let that go, can we?'

The Locomotive Bar, a big bar on LK Metro with a live band and chairs and tables outside, was a false alarm. This was the place where Kenny, Joey and Pete had had a big punch up with a bunch of farangs, a fight sparked off with them swiping other people's drinks from the tables. Jack wasn't involved, spending time on the island of Koh Samet with Minnie. But they stopped by and took a table and ordered a round of drinks. This time they would at least be paying for the drinks.

Joey, looking around the crowded bar: 'I can't see them anywhere.'

Kenny: 'There's a bunch of baldies over there. Isn't that them?'

Pete: 'No. That's not them.'

Joey: 'I reckon those twats were holidaymakers. Probably not here.'

Pete: 'No, they looked like expats to me.'

Kenny: 'How do you know?'

Pete: 'I was watching them. They seemed to be well used to this place. Like they lived here.'

Kenny, his face turning angry: 'There he is. There's that fucking Ladyboy.'

A big, hefty looking Ladyboy was serving drinks inside the bar.

Joey: 'Is that the one who kicked you with his heel?'

Kenny: 'Yes, that's him. I'm gonna have that fucker good and proper.'

Jack had heard enough. 'Look, Kenny, what are you gonna do? Okay, so there was a big fight here last year. Are you gonna let all that kick off again? What's the point?'

Kenny, looking sternly at Jack: 'The point is, Jack, vengeance. You don't let a cunt like that do you over and forget about it.'

Jack: 'And are you telling me that you were all blameless? Were you not doing something you shouldn't have been doing, like swiping drinks from the tables? What did you expect?'

Kenny turned away and glared at the Ladyboy.

Jack: 'Come on, lads, give it a rest. We've had this shit in Liverpool enough times. You end up fighting and then six months later you see the guys again and it all kicks off again. Where does it all end?'

Joey: 'You weren't here, Jack. You left us to go on an island with your girlfriend.'

Jack: 'Well, I'm here right now, Joey, and I'm having a good time and I don't want it ruined by us all ending up in a big fight. And besides, the blokes who you were scrapping with aren't even here.'

Enough was said on that matter. They had one drink in the bar and moved on.

It was a lively night in Pattaya and went by without a problem. The five men and Minnie went into a gogo bar, had a kebap and were about to call it a night when they were walking along Soi Buakow.

Joey: 'Let's have one for the road.'

Kenny: 'Find a nice little bar. I've heard enough live bands and all that shit.'

They walked along Soi Buakow looking for a bar to have one for the road. And then Pete stopped suddenly. He gazed into a large bar that was brightly lit. It looked like it was a small hotel with a walk-in bar below.

Pete: 'That's them.'

They all stopped and looked into the bar. There were no windows and they could see clearly inside. Only a few customers, but a group of men, typical middle aged farangs with bald heads, were seated at a corner table.

Joey: 'Where? Those four over there?'

Pete: 'Yes. That's them.'

Kenny, looking closely: 'Are they the ones we had the fight with last Christmas?'

Pete: 'Yes. Sure of it. I'd recognise them anywhere.'

They were silent for a moment. Problem with a place like Pattaya is that there are so many bald headed middle aged farangs that they all look the same. Then Joey said: 'You're right. That big cunt in the corner doing the talking. I'd recognise that twat anywhere. That's the cunt that knocked me out.'

Billy stood by and looked carefully at the four men sitting at the table in the corner. They all looked like big guys, but he wasn't afraid. Billy wasn't afraid of anything. 'Okay, lads,' Billy said with that now familiar malicious grin, 'I think we'd found our one for the road bar. This round's on me.'

Joey, Pete, Kenny and Billy went inside, but Jack, who wasn't present to witness the fight his mates had last time, hesitated and then took Minnie by the arm. He read the road ahead.

Jack, looking seriously at Minnie: 'Look, Minnie, here's some money for the taxi. I want you to go home now. I'm having a drink with my friends. You go straight home now and I'll see you tomorrow.'

Minnie, looking confused: 'But why? I want drink with you.'

Jack, sternly: 'No, Minnie. Don't argue. Go straight home now. Leave this area.' He kissed her. 'I'll see you tomorrow. Go, now.'

Minnie looked glum, but did as she was told. Jack watched her walk away until she was out of sight. He then went into the bar where the lads were.

Kenny, who had clocked Jack's talk to Minnie, said, 'Good move,

Jack.'

Jack nodded. Whatever was gonna happen here he didn't want Minnie involved with it.

A Thai waitress approached the men who were all standing at the bar. 'You want drinks, gentlemen?'

Billy: 'Yes, beers for everyone.' She swiftly brought them five beers. Billy handed her a one thousand baht note. 'I'm paying now. We are only having the one drink. So keep the change.'

The Thai women smiled with appreciation at the large tip. One thing the lads had noticed about Billy is that he was a generous tipper and seemed to have plenty of money.

The five men drank from their beer bottles for a few minutes, quietly observing the four men at the corner table. Joey remembered the voice of his enemy. The big, fat Yorkshireman who was doing all the talking. He was clearly the leader of the pack. Big fucker, too, even sitting down he looked big, and had the rough features and flat nose of a boxer. A right old bruiser. Joey was foolish to mess with him, and paid for it by the hardest punch he'd ever been hit with that could easily have broken Joey's face. You don't forgive or forget something like that.

Billy, to Joey: 'Is that him, Joey? That fat guy with the big mouth. Is that the one?'

Joey, nodding somberly: 'Yes, that's him alright. I'd recognise that voice anywhere.'

Billy, swigging his beer: 'Well, Joey, in that case I think it's time you said hello.'

Joey, alarmed: 'What?'

Billy, grinning: 'Go and say hello, Joey. He's your old friend, isn't he? Go on, Joey, go over there. Introduce yourself.'

Joey, looking scared: 'And what should I say?'

Billy: 'Well, think of something, Joey. You're a grown man. You don't need me to hold your hand. Just remember, Joey, I don't hold your hand, but I have got your back.'

I don't hold your hand but I have got your back. How eloquent, the lads thought. They were starting to warm to Billy.

Joey took a deep breath and a swig of beer: 'Okay,' he said, firming his body up. 'Okay, why the hell not?'

Joey walked over to the table where the four big men were seated. He was tense as fuck but wasn't going to back down now. He stopped at the table and all four men turned to look at him. The big bruiser was the leader but his henchmen looked like they could have a go as well. He thought for a moment that the last time he had had to flee from four big men wasn't so long ago. Then he was running for his life. Now, it was different. Now he wanted to get even.

Joey, to the four men: 'Alright, Gentlemen. Are you having a nice evening?' The four bald headed men looked up at him. And then they looked at each other. And then back to Joey. Joey didn't flinch. 'And what is the celebration, tonight, Gentlemen? Are you all members of the Yul Brynner Appreciation Society? Out on the town on a Slaphead night out?' There was laughter behind him from the lads at the bar. 'You know what, fellas, that would make a good horror movie title. Night Of The Slapheads.' More laughter. 'Of course, it would have to be an Egg certificate.'

The four bald headed men looked at each other again. And then back to Joey. Then the big leader of the bunch said, 'You're a fucking Scouser.' Joey noticed that his eyes were evil, sly and piggy.

Joey: 'I may be a fucking Scouser, but at least I have a full head of hair, and don't have a face like a Baboon's arse.'

More laughter from behind. Joey's audience were loving it.

Then one of the men said, 'I've seen you before. You were the ones who we were fighting with last Christmas.'

Then the big Yorkshire man nodded. 'Yes, I remember you. You better get out of my sight now, boy. I knocked you out last time. If I have to get up out of my seat I'll break you fucking neck.'

Joey raised his beer bottle to take a swig but the movement triggered off the big man, who sprung out of his chair and lurched at Joey. Joey stepped back quickly, remembering how hard this ogre could punch. The big Yorkshireman raised his clenched fist and was about to swing but suddenly realised Joey had been pushed aside and a big man, a big, fearsome looking man had replaced him.

Billy stood in front of the Yorkshireman, staring at him head on, standing tall and solid. The Yorkshireman suddenly realised he wasn't facing any lightweight, but being stared down by a big, strong looking, intimidating character, who looked like he'd had his fair share of battles.

There was a standoff between the two big men. You could have heard a pin drop at that moment. And then the big Yorkshireman said, 'Who the fucking hell are you?'

Billy smiled the malicious, sinister smile that had been known to put the fear of God into people. And then Billy said: 'I'm the ghost of Christmas Past. And I'm here to teach you a lesson, Mr Scrooge.'

You could hear the thud from across the bar as Billy headbutted the Yorkshireman, dropping him backwards across the table. Within seconds the bar erupted into violence. Shouting, shoving, punching, kicking. Billy laid into the big Yorkshireman with repeated, powerful blows to the face. The Yorkshireman's crew leapt out of their chairs to face their adversaries who were more than ready. Joey, Kenny, Jack and Pete, they were all tensed up and ready to battle. This was a time to get stuck in.

Kenny lurched at one of the men and they traded punches. Joey picked up a chair and whacked one of the baldies over the head. Pete was knocked to the floor by one of the men and was being kicked before Jack stepped in and wrestled the man to the floor before punching him repeatedly in the head.

'FUCKING BASTARDS!' one the men shouted after Joey had floored him with a chair and began kicking him in the head.

Meanwhile, there were shouts and screams from the girls behind the bar. A passerby popped his head in the door and said he was calling the police. The few other customers stepped as far back as they could to avoid flying chairs and bottles.

Kenny took a punch from one of the men but managed to stay on his feet, wrestling the man to the ground and slamming his head against the wall. Well, that was one less to worry about as he knocked the guy clean out.

And there was blood. And broken bottles and chairs and tables all over the place. Joey picked up a broken leg from a chair and began whacking any of the men who he could see, cracking bones and whatever else he could. Billy knocked another man to the floor with a powerful punch to the face. Then another lunged at him with a broken bottle in his hand. Billy shoved him to the ground and kicked him in the head until he was unconscious. Pete had recovered and began battering a man with a chair.

And then there was suddenly quiet. The shouting and screaming and racket of chairs and bottles and tables stopped, and the Liverpool men realised it was over. Billy kicked a man who groaned on the floor. And then they all stood around for a tense moment before realising it had ended. The four bald headed men were all lying sparked out on the floor, all of them bloodied. Jack looked to the big Yorkshireman who Billy had battered. He was out cold, barely recognisable, his face covered in blood. The other men were lying on the floor. Then Joey dropped his wooden weapon, Pete dropped the chair, Kenny and Jack looked at each other, both bleeding and wounded. And Billy, still on guard, looked around to see if any of the men could still pose a threat. No, none of them could. They were all knocked out on the floor.

Jack: 'Let's get out of here. Let's just go.'

They five men left the bar, noticing the shocked, horrified faces of the Thai waitresses.

Kenny, to the Thai bar staff: 'Sorry, girls, but they were the ones who started it.'

As they left the bar Jack took a backward glance at the aftermath of the brawl. It was an ugly sight, like as if someone had thrown a grenade in there. Broken tables and chairs and bottles, and four big men lying unconscious on the ground, blood splattered on their shirts. Not a pretty sight at all.

Before the five men could hastily disappear into the crowds down Soi Buakhao, Joey couldn't resist popping his head back into the doorway of the bar, pointing at the four battered men on the floor and grinning: 'I TOLD YOU NOT TO MESS WITH ME!'

CHAPTER EIGHT

GIRLS LIKE A BIT OF FUN, TOO

Lenny Pazazz: 'I don't want him on the show, Seamus. He has a bad reputation.'

Seamus, sitting next to Lenny in his bar: 'Well, we've agreed to it now, so it's too late.'

Lenny, grimacing: 'I wish I hadn't agreed to it. I barely know the man but others in Pattaya know all about him. Three other bar owners have approached me in the last few days and told me he's got a shady past, prison in the Netherlands for making..' Lenny got closer to Seamus to whisper the words, 'Kiddie porn.'

Seamus, wincing: 'Oh, there's no evidence of that. It's all just hearsay. The kind of shit that trolls like to put out. And remember, if he's shady he's not the only bar owner in Pattaya that is. There's plenty of them out there who have things to hide.'

Lenny Pazazz clearly wasn't happy about his guest this Friday night. But, he'd already agreed to interview Dutch Michael and have his Ladyboys perform on the show. He'd just have to grin and bear it.

Seamus: 'And besides, with the Youtube channel growing we need to get with the times. They're always accusing us of being sexist so I reckon having a few Ladyboys do a song and dance routine will be good for the show. It'll bring the woke element into it.'

Lenny Pazazz winced and drank his vodka and orange. Oh, well, he thought. Just have to go ahead with it. But somehow Lenny had a bad feeling about interviewing this man. Trouble attracts trouble.

VINNIE AND CAROL

While his mates were doing battle, Vinnie was curled up in bed again with Carol. He liked his hotel room and he liked shagging Carol. Okay she was a bit weighty, and a bit mouthy, and she was married, but what the hell? This is the best free fun he'd had in Pattaya.

Carol, playing with Vinnie's dick: 'Ahhh, isn't it great we met each other, Vinnie?'

Vinnie, beaming: 'Yeah, sure is.'

Carol: 'How's your mate doing?'

Vinnie: 'Joey?'

Carol: 'Yes. I suppose he's got another girl by now.'

Vinnie, bothered by Carol going on about Joey: 'Maybe. Haven't seen him since yesterday.'

Carol: 'I don't blame him for not going with Lizzy.'

Vinnie: 'Yes, you did mention that.'

Then Carol said, after a long pause: 'You know, if he hasn't found a girl, we can always invite him to join us.'

Somehow this didn't surprise Vinnie. Why didn't she just admit that she fancied. Joey?

Vinnie: 'You mean, for a threesome?'

Carol: 'Yes. Why not? I mean, we're on holiday, aren't we? We're supposed to be having fun...'

Vinnie, cutting in and rubbing Carol's tits: 'We are having fun.'

Carol: 'Yes, I know we are. But there's nothing wrong with inviting Joey to join us. I mean, I feel a bit guilty about trying to lumber him with Lizzy.'

Vinnie: 'Don't you feel guilty about Lizzy being without a fella.'

Carol: 'Oh, no. I mean, she's not gonna get anything here looking like that. I know Joey was pissed, but, you know. How about it?'

Vinnie would have been annoyed if he hadn't expected it. Carol had been mentioning Joey every five minutes, even when they were shagging. Now she wants a threesome with him and Joey. Oh, well, it was nice while that moment lasted. That moment that he felt it was him and only him that Carol fancied.

Vinnie: 'Okay, I'll mention it to him. Three in a bed. I think Joey will be up for that. He's a bit of a lad.'

Carol hugged Vinnie tightly: 'Ahhh, I knew you'd be cool with that. You, me and Joey. Three in a bed. What a lovely thought.'

THE LADS ARE WON OVER BY BILLY

The next morning, Jack, Joey, Kenny and Vinnie met in a Sports Bar in LK Metro. They were having an all English breakfast at a very good price. Just 199 THB for sausages, bacon, eggs, beans, black pudding, toast, coffee, the works. And it was good, hearty stuff. The talk was, predictably, about the big fight the night before. Vinnie was so excited to hear it. 'Fuck, I wish I'd been there,' he said.

As they were eating breakfast, the talk was all about Billy. If Billy's aim had been to win these guys over, to cement his friendship with them, then he had succeeded with flying colours. You must admit, we have all dreamed about being John Wayne or Clint Eastwood when, faced with a ruthless adversary, we have acted ultra cool and disposed of the villain with total confidence and style. Well, Billy was that character. No doubt about it. He was no 'all talk and no substance' impostor. Billy was the real deal, a real hard man who could deliver the coolest, most menacing words and then have the physical ability to deliver the violence. Billy talked the talk, then fought the fight. Fought fearlessly, ferociously, and with style. Billy was a gung ho, genuine macho man. And, yes, he had won these guys over.

Joey, munching his bacon on toast: 'Wow, you should have seen Billy go, Vinnie. I mean, what a hard man, what a fucking hard bastard.'

Kenny, also with a mouth full of breakfast: 'Fucking no fear at all. He's hard, alright.'

Jack: 'And he's cool. I mean, what was it he said before he pounded that big Yorkshire cunt?'

Joey, grinning: 'Awwww, that was so fucking cool, that was. I couldn't believe what I was hearing. He said, I'm the ghost of Christmas Past, and I'm here to teach you a lesson, Mr Scrooge. And then he battered fuck out of that fat cunt.'

Kenny, laughing: 'Fucking hell, I mean, that's straight out of a movie. How cool is that?'

Jack, nodding: 'Yeah, Dirty Harry would have been proud of that one.'

Vinnie, chomping on his sausage: 'Wow, I'd love to have seen that. Sounds like a hard bastard, alright. I'd say he's a good man to have on your side.'

They all agreed with that. A good man to have on your side. Only Jack was slightly disturbed by that thought. But he decided to keep his thoughts to himself, for now.

So the four men tucked into a very reasonably priced English breakfast and then decided what they were going to do for the day. Billy and Pete had gone somewhere, Jack had arranged to meet Minnie and Joey and Kenny were probably going to the beach. As for Vinnie, he seemed to be spending most of his time with that Brummy woman. The lads had never seen him so happy, whatever future he may have with her.

After the breakfast, they were going their separate ways when Vinnie had a quiet word with Joey outside the cafe.

Vinnie, talking quietly: 'Joey, I need to have a quiet word with you.'

Joey, looking curiously at Vinnie: 'As long as it doesn't involve that fucking whale from the other night.'

Vinnie: 'No, it's the other one. Carol.'

Joey, looking more curious: 'The one you've been shagging? What about her?'

Vinnie: 'She fancies you.'

Joey, grinning: 'What? She fancies...why, what has she said?'

Vinnie: 'Well, she kept mentioning you and I kind of figured it out.'

Joey wasn't surprised. He knew he was far better looking than Vinnie, so any girl that fancied Vinnie would fall head over heels for Joey. And, if he recalled, she wasn't that bad looking. Bit heavy, but worth a shag.

Joey: 'So what do you want me to do? She's your bird, isn't she?'

Vinnie, shaking his head: 'Not exactly. She's married, so there's not really a future. I'm just getting a free shag out of it.'

Joey, wondering where all this was going: 'So? What do you want me to do?'

Vinnie, deciding to get to the point: 'She wants a threesome, Joey. You, me and her. Three in a bed. She's up for it. So am I. So what do you reckon?'

Joey looked quizzically at Vinnie for a long moment. And then he burst out laughing.

Joey: 'What! A threesome, for fuck's sake. How about inviting her husband as well? The more the merrier.'

Vinnie: 'No, I'm serious, Joey. I mean, she goes to Gambia and those countries, she's had all that before. She's up for anything. She's on holiday, remember. She didn't want to come here but now she's getting shagged she wants to make the most of it.'

Joey, rolling his eyes, still laughing: 'Oh, fucking hell, I've heard everything now.'

Vinnie: 'You can't tell me you haven't done it before. This is Pattaya and anything goes here.'

Joey, laughing, grimacing and having a long thought, finally said: 'Okay, I'll do it. Three in a bed. Tell her I'm up for it.'

JACK AND MINNIE AT THE BEACH

Minnie liked going to the beach and renting one of those sunbeds. Jack couldn't figure out why they were called sunbeds when they were in the shade. Either way, he wasn't keen on lying on the beach. Gets boring very quickly. But he was with Minnie and he liked her company. So, the beach it was.

Minnie, lying back on the sunbed: 'Jack, why did you tell me to go away last night? What happened?'

Jack, expecting this: 'It's a long story, Minnie, and I didn't want you getting involved in it.'

Minnie: 'You fight? You have fight with someone?'

Jack: 'Something like that. Let's forget about it. We are here on the beach and that's all we need right now.'

Jack lay back thinking he had made a good move telling Minnie to go last night. What happened was something he didn't want her involved in, and also something he hoped wouldn't happen again. He hadn't come on holiday to get involved in any bar room brawls and, if you get involved in too many, it doesn't end well.

But Jack was disturbed. The fight had given the lads something to talk about, and Billy was now the star of the show. Yes, he'd won the guys over, alright. A big, fearsome movie hero is something we all look up to, want to be like, wish we could be like. And Billy had now established himself in the group. But where does this all end? Jack wondered. A good man to have on your side. That's what the lads were saying about Billy. Jack couldn't deny that Billy's intervention was like a guardian angel when he and Kenny had had that shit with the Thai men trying to scam them. He owed Billy for that. And Joey probably owed Billy for wreaking revenge on the man who'd knocked him out. So, yes, Billy was here and he was undoubtedly a good man to have on your side. But what side was this, exactly? Jack wondered. These were a group of Liverpool lads here in Pattaya to have a good time. Not here to be gangsters. Not here to make enemies. Not here to make war with anyone.

Truth was, Jack was more cynical than the others. While they now saw Billy as a gung ho hero, Jack was still suspicious. Something not quite right about Billy. But he'd keep his mouth shut for now. He didn't see any other option. Until something else happens.

GEORGE AND JEFF AT SOI HONEY

'Nice,' Jeff commented as he and George were walking up Soi

Honey. 'I can see why it's called Soi Honey. There's some right little darlings about here.'

George and Jeff walked slowly up the narrow Soi, taking in all the girls seated outside the massage parlours. Some nice ones, some not so nice and some very nice. Cuties all over the place. This was a great little Soi with massage parlours, hotels and a few bars with beers at sixty baht.

'Hellooooo, massage,' they heard from the smiling girls. Nice.

George: 'What's she doing with her mouth?'

Jeff: 'She's telling you what you can get if you go in there. Blowjob.'

George: 'Bit vulgar if you ask me.'

Jeff: 'Awwww, don't be a bore. You'll love it when you get in there.'

George: 'So, is that it? Massage and blowjob?'

Jeff: 'Not what I've heard. I've heard it's the full monty. Everything.'

George: 'You mean, you get a shag as well.'

Jeff: 'Everything. That's what I've been told. Massage, boom boom and happy ending. The works.'

George: 'Fucking hell. Well, what are we waiting for?'

They stopped at the HAPPY GIRLS massage parlour. There were about seven Thai girls seated outside. One of them, a good looking girl of about thirty, approached George. 'You like massage?' she grinned. George nodded and grinned back.

A cheeky little Thai girl of about twenty two approached Jeff. 'You like massage?' she said, grabbing his cock.

Jeff, taken aback: 'Ohhhhh, yes. I like it already.'

They were good looking girls and within minutes the deal for the massage and extras was made. The two married men took off their shoes and were led up the stairs to the massage rooms.

An hour later the two men were sitting at a bar a few doors down drinking sixty baht beers. They were both grinning.

George: 'Fucking hell, why did it take us so long to come here, Jeff?'

Jeff: 'I know what you mean. Tenerife has got nothing on this place.'

George: 'It's a good job Lizzy and Carol like sitting round the pool all day. They're well out of sight.'

Jeff: 'Well, to be honest, George, I'm past caring. Carol has been behaving very strangely since we've been here.'

George: 'I care. I'd care if Lizzy caught me. She's a violent woman. I've seen here temper and I don't want to see it again.'

Jeff: 'Well, that's up to you, George. The way I see it, if Carol continues treating me like dirt then we are gonna part company. I just have to make sure she doesn't get the house.'

George, frowning: 'Good luck with that.'

JOEY AND VINNIE IN A BAR

'I mean it,' Joey said as he and Vinnie were having a drink at a bar in Soi 13. 'If your dick is bigger than mine I'll fucking chin yer.'

Vinnie, grinning: 'Well, it is bigger than yours so you may as well do it now.'

The bar was the same one where they had first met Carol and her whale of a friend. A little bar in Soi 13. Neither of the two men knew quite what to make of all this.

Joey: 'So what exactly did she say? Did she just come straight out with it and say, 'Your mate's nice so let's have a threesome'?'

Vinnie nodded: 'Something like that.'

Joey: 'Sounds like a right slag.'

Vinnie: 'Well, suppose she is. But so what? It'll be a good laugh.'

Joey, nodding: 'It's nothing I haven't done before. What the fuck, at least we're not paying for it.' Then Joey had a thought. 'Wait a minute, maybe we should get her to pay us. I mean, she must pay those African fellas she's been banging in that, er, place she goes...'

Vinnie: 'Gambia.'

Joey: 'Yeah, that's it. And that fucking Moby Dick mate of her's must be paying a fortune for those poor bastards to shag her.' He looked up at the ceiling, in thought. 'I think we could be onto something here. How about you and me becoming a couple of gigolos for these sad western women who come here?'

Vinnie, also in thought: 'You know that's not a bad idea. But let's have a threesome first. I need a couple more beers before I'm in the right mood.'

Joey: 'Well, don't drink too many. Hey, wouldn't it be funny if you couldn't get a hard on and I can.'

Vinnie: 'Ha, fucking ha.'

At that moment Carol entered the bar, looking bright and cheerful. It was the first time Joey had really had the chance to take a good, sober look at her. And, he thought, although she was a bit heavy, she was not a bad looking blonde woman. She looked about fifty but she was quite shaggable. Very clean and well kept. Miles better than that monster of a mate of her's.

Carol, heading for the bar with a big smile: 'Hello, lads.' She turned to the barmaid and said, 'Vodka and orange for me and a couple of beers for these handsome young men here.'

Well, Joey thought, she certainly was a confident woman and had a way of putting men at ease. And seemed to be of a good nature. This was getting off to a good start.

A few drinks later and garrulous Carol said, 'Listen, boys. We are all adults here. So let's not be shy. Now where are we going to have some fun?'

Vinnie shrugged: 'Back to our hotel room, I suppose.'

Joey: 'It's gonna seem empty now that your mate isn't there to take up so much room.'

Carol, ignoring that one and pinching Joey's cheek with a big grin on her face: 'Don't worry, handsome. I know that wasn't a good experience with Lizzy, but I'll more than make it up to you.' She grinned, squeezing Joey's crotch. 'I'm more than enough woman for both of you.'

Joey and Vinnie looked at each other, and grinned. This was gonna be good. By the time the three of them had left the bar Joey had formed the opinion that Carol was a total slag. But so what? He was up for a good shag. Shag a slag. He liked the sound of that.

BILLY AND PETE

Billy loved playing with his Thai machete. He loved caressing it, practising the swishing movement in the mirror. This was his baby, and he was loving it. He also loved the black, silk kimono style costume he had bought. He'd worn it several times and observed himself in the mirror. He looked so cool, so sinister, so stylish. So terrifying. He couldn't wait to see the look of horror on everyone's face when he entered that bar. And, of course, he had an ace card up his sleeve.

But first Billy had to teach Pete how to look menacing with the knife. Billy was concerned at Pete's lack of enthusiasm for the knives, so they had to practise. Pete needed aggression and if it didn't come naturally then Billy had to teach him.

Billy, facing Pete in the hotel room: 'Hold that knife, Pete. Clasp it tightly. Raise your arm with it to look like you are about to stab someone.'

Pete, holding the knife nervously: 'Now what?'

Billy: 'Lunge at me, Pete. Lunge at me with the knife.'

Pete: 'You mean, you want me to stab you? I can't...'

Billy, sternly: 'Do it, Pete! You're supposed to look like a killer, not a nervous wreck.'

Pete, his palm sweating holding the knife: 'I can't. I can't stab you, Billy.'

Billy: 'I don't want you to stab me, Pete. I want you to lunge at me with it. I want to see some aggression out of you. Right now you are looking like a nancy boy. You need to look like a killer. You need to frighten people. Now lunge at me, with the knife, Pete. DO IT NOW!'

Pete, humiliated and scared, raised the blade high up and rushed towards Billy. Billy, surprisingly nimble for a big man, stepped backwards and allowed Pete to swing the blade into thin air. They both stopped for a moment and looked at each other. Then Billy smiled. 'You have that aggression in you, Pete. But you need to look more determined. You are not going to stab anyone. But you must look like you will if you need to. You have to look like you have the potential for violence. It's how you look, Pete. You need to look menacing. I think it could be an idea for you to wear a mask, Pete. A really evil, sinister looking one. Me, I don't need any mask. I know how to put the fear of God into people just by looking at them.'

Billy knew that his timid friend would need coaxing, but it was going to work. Billy was the natural leader and Pete was going to be his trusty sidekick. It was going to work

Later, Billy and Pete sat together on the balcony watching the sun going down. They were drinking coffee and Pete was quiet, as usual. Billy didn't mind. He could do enough talking for the two of them.

Billy: 'I think it's time we told the lads, Pete. What do you say?'

Pete, thinking for a moment: 'Tell them what? You mean, about the Dutchman on that show?'

Billy: 'Yes. It's only four days away and we should let them in on it. Don't want to spring it on them at the last minute.'

Pete, shaking his head: 'No, Billy. I don't think we should tell them.'

Billy: 'Why not? They're a good bunch of lads. I mean, look at the way we all fought together last night. Like we were a proper unit. We were good together, ruthless together. We stood side by side with each other. We're a good team. I think we should let them in on our plans.'

Pete, looking worried: 'I'm not sure, Billy.'

Billy, quizzically: 'What are you not sure about? They are a good group of lads. Do you not trust any of them?'

Pete, thinking for a moment: 'Well, still not sure. I mean, having a big fight is one thing. We've done that before. But murdering someone…I don't know.'

Billy, looking perturbed: 'It isn't murder, Peter. It's justice. That evil man did you wrong, left you in a bad, disturbed mental state. Led to your breakdown. He deserves to pay the ultimate price for that. And, besides, it's not the lads who will be chopping that fucker's head off. I'm the one who will have the

pleasure of that.'
  Pete: 'It's just that…some of them…I'm not so sure.'
  Billy: 'Which ones? Who is it you cannot trust?'
  Pete: 'Jack. I'm not so sure about Jack.'
  Billy: 'Jack? He's alright, isn't he? What is it about Jack you're unsure about?'
  Pete: 'Well, he's…I dunno. Mr fucking sensible, that's what he is. Always thinks he's got his head screwed on better than the rest of us.'
  Billy, raising his eyebrows: 'Jack? Really? Jack, eh. So Jack is the one who could be a liability.'

CAROL, JOEY AND VINNIE

It was a hoot. An absolute hoot. From the moment Carol stepped naked out of the bathroom it was a hoot. She was plump but full of personality and really brought out the fun in Joey and Vinnie. They were all laughing. Trousers dropped, clothes came off, Carol was picked up by Vinnie and thrown laughing on the bed, Joey was having a wank looking at them going at it, then it was his turn and…..you can guess the rest.
  Afterwards, the three of them were in bed, Carol sandwiched in between the two men.
  Carol: 'Fucking hell, who'd have thought? Who'd have thought when we came here that we'd be having three in a bed? And I thought this place was shit.'
  Joey, grinning: 'Well, I thought it was pretty shit but it's funny how life turns out.'
  Vinnie: 'I like Pattaya. It's full of surprises. More than what you expect.'
  Carol, grabbing both men's dicks: 'You have such a way with words, Vinnie. And as for you, Joey, you are a real superstud. Aren't you glad you joined us?'
  Joey, grinning: 'Fucking great.' He and Vinnie high fived as Carol lay in between them, playing with their private parts. 'I'd

say we make a damn good little team.'

JACK AND MINNIE

This was very bad news, Jack thought. Very bad. He needed to hear it again to make sure he'd heard right.

Jack was in the hotel room that evening with Minnie. He was watching YouTube on his laptop. He'd done a fair bit of research on Thailand by watching videos and he'd gotten used to some of the channels. One of the channels was called Thailand News Today. It was a channel run by an Australian guy who read news stories of what was happening in Thailand, and had info about visas and rules and some regional news stories. He was watching today's episode when he heard something that he didn't like the sound of. So he picked up his laptop and took it into the bedroom to rewind the news video and hear it again.

Minnie was in the main room and saw Jack going into the bedroom, looking a bit concerned. 'What is wrong?' she said.

Jack: 'Nothing. I'm just going in here for a minute. I'll be with you soon.'

Jack put the laptop down on the bed and rewound the video to watch it again. He sat down on the bed, worried. This didn't sound good at all. He found the section he was looking for and played it again.

The Australian man read the news report that had just come in.

'Police are looking for a group of men who were involved in a bar room brawl last night in the Soi Buakhao area of Pattaya. Police are treating this as a serious incident which has left one man in a critical condition on a life support machine. It is believed the group of men, said to be five of them, are from the city of Liverpool in England. Any witnesses to the incident should report it to the Pattaya police. We'll give you more details of that report when we get them.'

Jack sat back on the bed and switched off the video. He stared blankly at the wall for a moment, and then said, 'Ohhhhhhh, shit.'

CHAPTER NINE

WITH FRIENDS LIKE THESE...

Lenny Pazazz: 'Well, I hope you are all having a great week in the entertainment capital of Thailand. Just remember Friday's fun filled show in which we'll have music, lovely ladies and some special guests including Michael, who will be telling us about his new Ladyboy nightclub which is soon to be open. And he's bringing along some of his delightful cast. You don't want to miss that.'

Michael watched the short YouTube promo clip on his smartphone. He had to hand it to Lenny Pazazz, he was well organised with his bars and his YouTube channel and his live shows. Like many, Micheal found him to be annoying, like a Seventies DJ who has the corniest jokes and the cheesiest, MR Clean personality. But he was good at what he did and had offered Michael a helping hand. It was actually Seamus, Lenny's sidekick and shareholder in the bars, who had gotten Michael and his Ladyboys an appearance on the show. And, with just a week to go before the opening of his Ladyboy cabaret show, Michael really needed that publicity.

The rehearsals were going well, and Micheal had some of the most glamorous Ladyboys lined up for the show. It was all going to plan, no hiccups. As Michael sat and watched the guys in rehearsals while drinking his coffee, he thought that pretty soon he would have a lively new business venture on his hands and be able to put the disaster of the previous year behind him. He sipped his coffee and thought for a moment about that night when the Liverpool men had caused trouble at his

SM club and frightened his wealthy customers away and caused the police to close his club down. They even stole his expensive camera which he had used to make SM porn with. Bastards. He wondered where they were now. He wondered if they would ever show their face in Pattaya again. Well, if they did, Michael didn't want to hear from them again.

He sipped his coffee and thought: fucking Scousers.

CAROL AND LIZZY BESIDE THE POOL

Carol and Lizzy were lounging beside the pool. Weather still fantastic in Thailand. Back home in Birmingham it was cold, wet, awful. This was paradise so let's enjoy it.

Lizzy: 'So where have you been swanning off to recently?'

Carol, lying back and grinning: 'I've been having fun. The kind of fun I would have had if we'd gone to Gambia.'

Lizzy: 'So you're still shagging that Vinnie bloke?'

Carol: 'Better.'

Lizzy: 'What? Don't tell me you've moved on from him and have found another dick.'

Carol, sitting up and slurping at her strawberry cocktail: 'It's actually two dicks I've found.'

Lizzy: 'Two dicks? You mean…I know. You're shagging that other prat as well. Fucking knew it. Some fucking friend you are.'

Carol, taking another slurp: 'Liz, you would have done the same thing. I mean, there's fuck all else on offer here right now. May as well take what you can get.'

Lizzy was disgusted. Not with her friend's behaviour but with her betrayal. 'Well, I'm getting fuck all here. Has that Joey fella said anything about me? If he has I'll rip his fucking poncey head off.'

Carol: 'He hasn't said anything about you. In fact, he's quite nice, really.'

Lizzy: 'Nice? I suppose it's nice having two dicks at the same time. Well, good for you. But I'd watch that one if I were you. Looks a sly bastard. I'd watch the pair of them, come to that. Fucking Scousers. They'll rob you blind if you give them the chance. Well, don't come crying to me if that happens.'

Lizzy was depressed. She was having a shit time here. Never wanted to come to Thailand. Nothing here for her. And now, with her best mate shagging two fellas and her with nothing but her useless little shit of a husband, she was as miserable as sin. And just where was he swanning off to, come to that?

Lizzy was watching TV in the hotel room when George entered the room. She looked him up and down as he walked in and made his way to the bathroom. He was grinning. Yes, he was grinning.

Lizzy: 'Where have you been all day?'

George, peeing: 'I've been having a wander round with Jeff. Nice place, Pattaya. Nice beach and all that?'

Lizzy: 'So is that where you've been? The beach?'

George: 'Yes. The beach?'

Lizzy: 'Did you go for a swim?'

George: 'Nahhh, just had a walk and sat down on a bench. Then we had a couple of beers in a beach bar.'

Lizzy: 'Oh, yes. Which one?'

George; 'Can't remember what it was called. Lots of tourists there.'

Lizzy: 'Well, tomorrow you can take me there. I'm pissed off hanging around here all day.'

George, coming out of the bathroom and still grinning: 'Anything for you, my sweet.'

Lizzy continued to watch TV. George was grinning like a Cheshire Cat. Lizzy began wondering. If what she was thinking was correct, she'd tear his fucking bollocks off.

JACK AND KENNY

Jack went to see Kenny first. This was very bad news and Kenny was the one who he could trust most with bad news. He knocked on Kenny's hotel room door. Kenny let him in. It was afternoon and Kenny was hung over from the night before. His girl had gone home so they could talk freely.

Jack, looking anxious: 'Kenny, you've got a smartphone. Switch Youtube on. There's something I have to show you.'

Kenny, noticing Jack's anguish: 'What is it?'

Jack: 'Switch it on, Kenny. I'll show you what it is. And it's bad news. Very bad.'

Kenny, fumbling about with his smartphone: 'Youtube. Now what?'

Jack: 'Type into the search, Thailand News Today.' Kenny typed it in. It came up with a selection of videos including one dated a couple of hours ago. 'That one. Click on that and then fast forward it to about 8 minutes.' Kenny clicked on the video and fast forwarded it. The Australian man appeared on the screen. 'Listen to this, Kenny.'

They listened together. It was the section beginning with, 'Police are looking for a group of men...' Kenny's mouth dropped open. He turned to Jack. Neither of them spoke for a moment.

Jack: 'It's about us, Kenny. Can't be anyone else.'

Kenny: 'Fuck. What are we gonna do?'

Jack: 'I haven't decided. But I reckon the police are gonna be knocking on the door soon. We may have to get on the move.'

Kenny: 'Do the others know about this?'

Jack: 'No. I haven't told them. Kenny, this is something we have to think very carefully about. Can't make any rash decisions. One of those guys is on a life support machine. That's serious.'

Kenny: 'Who do you reckon that could be.'

Jack: 'Kenny, we were all doing our bit during that fight. Everything got a bit blurred. But I reckon it could be that big Yorkshire fella, the one Billy was battering fuck out of.'

Kenny: 'He was the ringleader out of that lot.'

Jack: 'Yes. I can't say exactly what happened, but I remember Billy really going at it hard. I mean, Billy is a powerful guy.'

Kenny: 'He's a fucking psycho.'

Jack: 'Did you see Billy really going over the top when he was beating that guy?'

Kenny: 'Fucking right I did. Billy was whacking him and whacking him non-stop. Even when that big guy went on the floor, Billy was still jumping on his head.'

Jack, looking up at the ceiling: 'Fuck. I didn't see that, but it doesn't surprise me. I mean, if that guy is on a life support...and he was to die...'

Kenny: 'Billy would be done for manslaughter.'

Jack: 'Maybe we'd all be done for manslaughter.'

Kenny: 'You reckon?'

Jack: 'This is Thailand, Kenny. We don't know the script with the laws out here. For all we know they could bang us all up in the Bangkok Hilton until they make their minds up what to do with us.'

JACK, KENNY, JOEY AND VINNIE

Of the six Liverpool men, they were staying in three different hotels. Jack and Kenny, Joey and Vinnie, Pete and Billy. The first four men were the ones who would get together to discuss anything. Pete and Billy seemed a bit out of it, inseparable friends from a loony bin.

So Jack, Kenny, Joey and Vinnie were together in a bar complex on Beach Road drinking the usual happy hour beer. Jack was the one to break the news to Joey and Vinnie.

Vinnie: 'What? Who is in intensive care? I mean, I wasn't there so it doesn't involve me.'

Joey, taking a swig of his beer: 'Do they know which one is on the life support?'

Jack: 'We don't know yet. But Billy was whacking fuck out of that big guy. We reckon it's him.'

Joey, his face cracking into a smile: 'Really?' Then Joey sat back and laughed out loud. He banged the table in triumph. 'Yes! Serves the cunt right. I knew I'd get my own back on that fat cunt. Life support machine, eh? Awwww, my heart goes out to him.'

Jack and Kenny looked at each other, then Jack began shaking his head. Typical Joey.

Jack, looking serious: 'Joey, I'm very pleased you got your revenge, but this is no laughing matter. This is serious. We are in the shit, mate. Serious shit.'

Kenny: 'If that cunt dies we could all be done for manslaughter.'

Joey, still grinning: 'Manslaughter? Ohhh, fucking give over. You don't believe that, do you? And besides, it wasn't me who whacked fuck out of him. Billy did that.'

Vinnie, looking perturbed: 'Well, I wasn't involved. If they've got CCTV anywhere they won't see me on it.'

Jack grimaced and looked out onto the activity of Beach Road, Pattaya. Typical Vinnie. Not a sincere bone in his body. Yesterday he was sharing the excitement of the fight and saying something like, 'I wish I was there'. Now, it's turned sour and he doesn't want any part of it. Typical, fickle Vinnie.

Joey: 'Do Pete and Billy know about this yet?'

Kenny shook his head: 'No, we haven't told him.' He looked at Jack again. 'Do you think we should tell the other two, Jack?'

Jack shook his head: 'No. I mean, I don't know. This is all a bit much.'

Kenny: 'Well we'll have to tell them sooner or later. I mean, Billy's the one who may have gone a bit too far. He needs to know.'

Jack shrugged: 'I just don't know. Can't imagine what Billy's reaction to this would be. I mean, what are we getting into here? Yesterday you all said he's a good man to have on your side. What side is this, exactly? I came here on holiday. I came here to have a good time, not to put anyone on a life support machine.'

Kenny waved to the Thai girl to order a new round of drinks. The atmosphere at the table had become very sombre. And then Vinnie said, 'I think Billy's not a full shilling.' The others looked at him. 'Of course, don't tell him I said that.'

Jack: 'I think we are all thinking the same thing, Vinnie.'

CAROL, JEFF, LIZZY AND GEORGE

To an observer, it looked like a typical British foursome having a meal in a Thai restaurant in Pattaya. Not a cheap restaurant, either. It was a big seafood restaurant in Walking Street, the main touristy area of Pattaya.

Jeff, grimacing as he read the menu: 'Fuck me, this is expensive. I thought Thailand was supposed to be cheap.'

George: 'Ay, you're not wrong there. Looks like a ripoff. Shall we go somewhere else?'

Carol: 'Ohhhhhh, typical fucking tight arses, aren't you both? What was it you said about, 'let's go to Thailand, it's all cheap there'?'

Lizzy: 'Well, I'm happy here and I fancy the cod. I don't want all this fancy stuff. Just cod, chips and peas. Proper meal.'

George, looking at the menu; 'Even Cod chips and peas isn't cheap here. Are you sure we've got the right country here?'

Carol: 'Oh, stop your fucking whinging. I'll have the cod and chips as well if it makes you happy.'

They all settled for cod and chips, British style. It was a nice restaurant, plush with a sea view. And the cod and chips was nice. But it wasn't a happy foursome night out. Nobody trusted anybody here. Jeff had an idea Carol was cheating on him. Lizzy had an idea that George was cheating on her. Carol would rather have been sandwiched between Joey and Vinnie. Lizzy wished she was in Gambia.

It was a strange set up.

SIX MEN AND A SECRET

Pete and Billy joined the others in the bar on Beach Road. It was late afternoon and Kenny had messaged Billy. Pete didn't have a mobile phone. Pete didn't have anything.

'How are you, warriors?' Billy beamed as he took a seat at the table with Jack, Kenny, Joey and Vinnie. Pete, his lap dog, sat next to Billy.

Jack: 'Hi, Billy. We're just getting another round of drinks. You having the usual?'

Billy, settling into his chair: 'Yes, same for us.'

They all had a round of drinks. Now it was time to talk serious.

Jack: 'Billy, we've got some news for you. And it doesn't sound good.'

Billy, taking a swig of beer and raising his eyebrows: 'Bad news? Go ahead. I'm listening.'

Jack glanced at others, who were waiting for him to do the talking: 'Billy, that big fight we had the other night. We believe the police are looking for us.'

Pete, his mouth falling open: 'What?'

Billy, unperturbed: 'Keep going, Jack. Give us the rest.'

Jack: 'It's been in the Pattaya news. A big fight in Soi Buakow has left one man in a critical condition, life support machine. We reckon it's the big guy who you flattened.'

Billy, taking another swig and looking thoughtful: 'Is this fact? How do you know all this?'

Kenny: 'It's on YouTube. I can show it to you if you want.'

Billy: 'And you know the guy who is on a life support is the fat bastard who I laid out?'

Jack: 'Just a hunch, Billy. You gave him a good hiding.'

Billy: 'But you've no concrete facts about anything?'

Jack, thinking this wasn't gonna be easy: 'This news report says police are looking for five men involved in a bar room brawl in Soi Buakhao. Someone has reported us as being from Liverpool. And one man is on a life support. We have heard any updates yet.'

They were all quiet for a tense moment. Billy looked intently at his beer bottle. Even saying nothing he could be quite scary. You never knew what this guy was gonna do next.

Billy: 'So you've nothing more to add, Jack?'

Jack, who seemed to have been nominated as the spokesman, shrugged.

Billy, taking a long swig from his beer bottle and placing it down loudly on the table: 'So you are the spokesman in the group, Jack? You're the one that decides things for the others?'

Jack, a bit taken aback: 'No. What makes you say that? I mean, we thought we'd better tell you. The police are looking for us and everyone needs to be informed.'

Billy, looking angry: 'But I notice you're the one who does the talking. Do I detect a bit of hostility towards me, Jack? I'm new to the gang and you don't quite trust me yet?'

Jack, Kenny, Joey and Vinnie all looked at each other.

Kenny: 'We trust you, Billy. You sorted that guy out good and proper the other night and he deserved it. Good on you.'

Billy, not letting Jack off the hook: 'But do you feel the same way, Jack? Are you the influencer here? Is it the case that the rest of the lads here think I'm alright but you are the cynical one? You don't trust me, and you're putting the word to the others that I'm not to be trusted?'

Jack, thinking this wasn't going well: 'Billy, I've nothing against you. I'm just reporting a situation we are in and we all need to talk about it. Decide what we should do.'

Billy: 'And what are you going to do, Jack? Are you going to desert the lads like you did last year?'

Jack, alarmed, looking at Pete: 'What?'

Billy: 'I've heard all about it, Jack. When the lads were in the shit last year, you disappeared to an island with your little bar girl, leaving them to face all kinds of hostility in a strange land. Some friend you are, aren't you, Jack?'

Jack was taken aback, and, to be truthful, quite scared. It was clear Pete had been putting the knife in. Joey and Vinnie had no comment. So it was left to Kenny to come to Jack's defence.

Kenny: 'Billy, Jack is not a deserter. He helped rescue Pete from that weirdo place last year. And have you forgotten, he fought alongside us the other night. He's not a deserter.' Kenny then looked at Pete. 'Isn't that right, Pete?'

Pete, grimacing: 'He deserted us last year when we needed him.'

Kenny, thinking Pete was acting like a twat: 'Okay, so he went to an island coz we all fell out. But he sure as hell didn't desert you when you'd been kidnapped. Have you told Billy that bit, Pete? The bit about how Jack, and the rest of us, played a big part in rescuing you from that SM club and that evil Dutch cunt.'

Billy nodded: 'Oh yes, Pete has told me all about that.'

Kenny, not letting Pete off the hook: 'Look, Billy, I know Pete is your friend. But he's my friend as well. In fact, I've known Pete all my life. And when he tells you about what owlarses his mates can be he doesn't always give you the full picture. Now has Pete told you about how we all risked our lives - all of us, me, Jack, Joey, Vinnie, all of us - when we rescued him from that club? Pete owes us for that.'

Billy, grimacing: 'You mentioned the Dutch cunt. What do you know about him?'

Joey, finally speaking: 'Pervert, like all them weirdos.'

Kenny: 'Pervert with a big camera. I knocked him out with a champagne bottle.'

Billy, finally smiling again: 'That's good. Yes, that's good, Kenny.' He then turned to Pete. 'Is is time to tell them, Pete?'

All the lads seemed perturbed by now. Tell us what? They all thought. This was going from bad to worse.

Pete, shaking his head: 'No. Not yet.'

Billy: 'Why, Pete? Do you not think we can trust all your friends?'

No one was brave enough to say, 'tell us what?'

Pete, looking out of it: 'We'll tell them later.'

Billy looked at the boys, Jack, Kenny, Joey and Vinnie. Then he smiled and said, 'I think me and Pete should retreat for now. We've got work to do.'

Minutes later, Pete and Billy had drank their beers and left the bar. The other four breathed a sigh of relief. With Billy you got the feeling that any second it could all explode into violence.

Kenny: 'Well, at least we told them.'

Joey: 'So now everybody knows. The police are looking for us. What next?'

Jack shrugged: 'I'm none the wiser. I think we should just sit back and listen to the next news report. Hope for the best.'

At least Jack had learned one thing. Pete had a spiteful streak aimed at him and Billy was a highly dangerous man if you got on the wrong side of him. And Jack thought he may just have got on the wrong side of him. Thanks, Pete.

JACK AND KENNY

Jack and Kenny were on the town together that night. They needed to talk. With Pete and Billy spending most of their time together and Joey and Vinnie having a threesome with Carol, it was left to Jack and Kenny to come up with an idea. They had a problem, a cloud looming in the background. And they were the only two who seemed to take it seriously.

Jack, standing next to Kenny in a bar on Walking Street: 'What if that guy dies, Kenny?'

Kenny, swigging his beer: 'Then we're in the shit.'

Jack: 'Why is it that no one else is taking this too seriously?'

Kenny: 'They'll take it seriously if he dies and we all end up in the Bangkok Hilton.'

Jack: 'That's what I mean. Well, at least we've told the others about it. We've done our part.'

Kenny: 'What do you reckon, Jack? She we get the fuck out of here, go to Bangkok?'

Jack: 'If the police are looking for us then we are not going to get out of this country. They either nab us here or at the airport.' Jack shook his head in dismay. 'To be honest, I can do without any cloak and dagger stuff. I recall this was just you and me on holiday together. I kind of liked it that way.'

Kenny, nodding: 'Me, too.'

Jack: 'And what about Pete and Billy? That's a strange friendship, isn't it?'

Kenny, grinning: 'You're not suggesting….?'

Jack, shrugging: 'I'm not really bothered. I'm past caring. But what I would like to know is what is it that Billy wanted to tell us.'

Kenny: 'What?'

Jack: 'Remember, when we were in the bar today. Billy said something about 'shall we tell them', and Pete said no. What was that all about?'

Kenny, grinning more: 'Maybe they are shagging each other. Maybe that's what Billy wanted to tell us.'

Jack, shaking his head and looking serious: 'No. I don't think that's it. I think it's something else. I think they are planning something together. Something them two are thinking about but not telling us about, not sure if they can trust us.'

Kenny: 'What on Earth makes you say that?'

Jack: 'It's just a hunch I have.'

BILLY AND PETE

Billy put his silk kimono on and stood in front of the mirror. He held the machete and practised his swing.

Billy: 'Swoosh…..swoooosh….Swoooooosh….'

Pete was watching Billy from the balcony. Billy was an imposing figure, but scary. Very scary.

Billy: 'Come and join me, Pete. It's time you practised a few moves..'

Pete left the balcony and stood near Billy, awaiting his next order. 'What do you want me to do?'

Billy, staring at his own reflection with the machete in hand: 'Go and get those knives out of the case, Pete. I want you to practise handling them.'

Pete, frowning: 'I've already done a bit of practise with them.'

Billy: 'You need to get used to them. It's not just a case of picking a knife up and stabbing people. You need to get used to the grip, wave it about, threaten people with it, look frightening with the knife in your hand.'

Pete did as he was told. He took the biggest knife from the suitcase where they had it hidden away from maids, and held it up. It sure was a beauty. But, Pete thought, what am I supposed to do with it? What is really gonna happen? This just isn't me.

Billy continued swooshing the machete in the mirror, and then finally, put it down on the bed. He indicated for Pete to put the knife down beside the machete, and then said: 'Let's go out on the balcony, Pete. It's beer time. You and me need to talk.'

So they opened a couple of beers and sat down together on the balcony, overlooking a fine view of Pattaya.

Billy, taking a gulp of Singha beer and looking out at the view: 'Are you afraid, Pete?'

Pete, lying: 'No.'

Billy: 'Look, Pete. If our friendship is going to be solid then you need to tell me the truth. So I'll ask you again. Are you afraid?'

Pete, thinking long about his answer: 'Yes. Yes, Billy, I'm afraid. I don't know how I can cope with this. It just isn't me.'

Billy, turning to Pete's worried face: 'And would you be braver if you had the others with you? You still haven't told me if you want the others, your friends, in on our plan.'

Pete, shaking his head: 'No, it wouldn't work. I just think they would fuck the whole thing up.'

Billy: 'Why is that? Can you not trust them? Is it Jack you can't trust?'

Pete: 'Yes. I mean, I wouldn't trust Jack. After the way he deserted us last year, I wouldn't trust him.'

Billy: 'And what about Joey?'

Pete: 'Joey? Nahh, he's unreliable. He's an Owlarse. Same as Vinnie. They'd say it's a good idea and then have a change of plan. Probably wouldn't even turn up.'

Billy: 'That leaves Kenny. You know, I like Kenny. He's a bit of a tiger. Didn't he say he smashed a bottle of champers over that Dutch cunt's head?'

Pete nodded: 'Yes, Kenny's alright. But he's a mate of that twat Jack. And I don't think he'd be up for this. It's not Kenny's style.'

Billy, looking down: 'You say you can't trust these people but they are the ones who came to your rescue last year. All of them, even Jack.'

Pete: 'Nah, this is different. Then they were rescuing their mate. But this…this is way out of their league. They wouldn't have any part in this.'

Billy downed his bottle of beer and gazed out at the early evening Pattaya sky. 'Okay, then, Pete, that leaves just you and me. We'll forget about the others. But, you know what, Pete? We don't need them. Just you and me will be enough. I've got it all planned.'

Pete swigged his beer and then stood up and began pacing around the balcony. He looked anguished, scared.

Pete: 'But what's going to happen, Billy? I mean, what's really gonna happen?'

Billy, noticing his friend's anguish and standing up to put a hand on his shoulder: 'What's gonna happen, Pete, is that we are going to get famous.'

Pete, stopping pacing and looking Billy straight in the eyes: 'Famous? Is that what you call it?'

Billy, looking intently at his friend: 'Yes, famous, Pete. And not all for the wrong reasons.'

Pete: 'But it's murder, Billy. Cold blooded murder. And we'll go to prison for it. One of those foul, horrible Thai prisons. That's where we'll be spending the rest of our lives.'

Billy, shaking his head with a grin: 'No, Pete. You're wrong. We will not be spending the rest of our lives in prison. In fact, we won't be there for very long.'

Pete: 'What makes you say that?'

Billy: 'Because of public support, Pete. Public support. Public outcry, you could call it. You see, we are not beheading an innocent man. Oh, no, far from it. You have seen the comments on the internet about this Dutch Michael. People know about him. He is a bad man. Evil. He has served time in a Dutch prison for child pornography offences, he is believed to be involved in trafficking and abusing underage girls and boys. He is wanted for questioning by police forces in other countries. He's a bad man. For fuck's sake, Pete, I don't need to tell you how bad he is. You yourself were a victim of this evil, vile rattlesnake. And people know about him. People around the world who use the internet know all about this monster. They want him brought to justice, but the world is so corrupt and justice is so weak that rattlesnakes like this get away with these crimes all the time. They know how to bribe and blackmail the right people. They know how to cover their tracks.'

Pete looked down at the floor and listened to Billy. This man could talk sense. And he was right, Pete himself had been a victim of this rattlesnake. God knows what would have become of him if the others hadn't rescued him.

Billy: 'So this is where we come in, Pete. The public out there want heroes. They want heroes like us to come and do what the authorities of this world are too spineless to do. They want us to deliver proper justice to the evil men of this world. And, Pete, when that Dutch cunt's head rolls about the floor of that bar, leaving a trail of blood and brains, the people around the world will be cheering. That video clip will go viral. It will be one of the most famous, infamous videos of all time. And we will be the heroes, Pete, you and me.'

Pete: 'But we'll go to prison, Billy.'

Billy, still grinning: 'But not for long, Pete. Like I said, we have public support. No sooner will the cell doors close on us then there will be people around the world who will be campaigning for our release. People will say we did a marvellous thing, ridding the world of that evil scum. They will demand an early release for us, and many will say we should be given medals for our bravery.'

Pete listened. And he listened. Billy was so persuasive that Pete could only listen.

Billy, satisfied he was getting through to Pete: 'Don't worry about prison, Pete. I'm going to be there to protect you. You'll come to no harm while I'm there. And then, when we come out, that is when our fame will truly begin. Do you know what will happen when we come out of prison, Pete?'

Pete, shaking his frightened head: 'What?'

Billy, smiling: 'Fame, Pete, fame. The whole world will want to know our story. We are the gladiators who beheaded the evil scum. People around the world will love us for it. We will write books, people will write books about us, they will make documentaries about us. We will be invited on chat shows. Imagine that, Pete. Imagine you and me wearing smart suits going onto prime time TV and telling our story about how we wanted to make an example of the evil child abusing scum of this world. We will say we were sick of the weak justice of this world so we decided to deal out a bit of justice of our own. And they will applaud us, Pete. You and me will be standing side by side on TV while the audience gives us spontaneous applause. And, of course, we will be paid handsomely for all our media appearances.'

Pete, his head lifting up when he heard the mention of money: 'How much do you think we can make?'

Billy, knowing that bit would work: 'Lots, Pete. Lots of money. TV appearances, book deals, documentary interviews. Who knows, maybe we'll even be able to sell the film rights. Pete, you and I will be millionaires.'

Pete nodded. Millionaires, would we be? TV shows, documentaries, book deals. Pete contemplated making a joke about charging for cutting the ribbon to open a new local supermarket, but he decided against that one.

Billy looked intently into Pete's eyes and hugged him tightly. 'Pete, you must realise that this is OUR moment. This is our fifteen minutes of fame. It is a once in a lifetime moment and we must seize it with both hands.'

Pete listened to Billy and, strangely enough, Billy made sense to him. All as Pete knew is he had nothing left going for himself in life and had almost lost the will to live. Either way, there was no backing out now. The Lenny Pazazz show was just two days away. And he and Billy were going to gatecrash the party.

CHAPTER TEN

BLACKMAIL

Lee was happy. He hadn't been so happy since he first met Ning a couple of years ago. Of course, he'd had his doubts. Friends had told him to be careful and not to send her money. Yes, he'd heard the stories of her probably having other sponsors. Friends said she could be taking him for a mug. And, yes, when he arrived in Pattaya this time and she seemed to be ignoring his calls and texts, he'd thought the worst. That he'd made a big mistake in trusting her, and that his friends had tried to warn him. And, yes, for a brief while, he had felt very hurt and very foolish. But that was all over now. Lee and Ning were now together in a bar in Soi Diamond and they were sitting beside each other like a couple of lovebirds and it was a lovely night and the beer was cold and the music was good. Lee had decided his beloved, beautiful Ning was the one for him. Forget about the doubters, Ning was his girl and he was so happy to be with her.

Unfortunately for Lee, some bastard was about to throw a spanner in the works.

'You want another drink, love?' Lee said as hugged Ning.

'Yes. Another vodka orange.'

Lee ordered another drink for him and Ning. It was such a good night they were having. The bar wasn't too busy or too noisy, just a nice atmosphere in one of the side Sois off Walking Street. And when the Thai waitress brought their drinks, Lee and Ning, sitting close together, clinked glasses and Lee said, 'To us.'

Ning, smiling serenely into Lee's eyes: 'To us.'

Lee kissed Ning again and hugged her tightly. Then a loud angry voice came out of nowhere:

'OHHHH, SO THIS IS WHAT YOU'RE ALL ABOUT THEN, IS IT?'

Lee and Ning turned to see a tall, angry looking man staring down at them. His voice sounded German.

Tomas, to Ning: 'So this is why you've been ignoring me for the last week. Is this another one of your sponsors? Or are you just trying to get him on board as well?'

Lee, angrily: 'Who the fuck are you?'

Tomas, turning to Lee: 'I'm another one of her sponsors. How about you? How much money do you send her each month?'

Lee: 'What's it to you?'

Tomas, to Ning: 'Well, Ning, is he another of your sponsors? So how much does this one send you each month?'

Ning didn't flinch. She was a tough girl and not easily intimidated. She looked blankly at Lee, then back to Tomas and said: 'He pay a lot more than you do.'

Lee's mouth fell open. He looked at Ning. Then he looked at Tomas. And then Lee became angry. He released his embrace from Ning, grinding his teeth.

Lee, glaring at Tomas: 'You…better get the fuck out of here!'

Tomas, unflinching: 'Oh, don't worry, I'm going. But first I want my money back. You have been deceiving me for the last two years, Ning, and it has cost me a lot of money. So, twenty thousand baht a month, for just over two years. I make that about five hundred thousand baht you owe me. So if you can pay me that money, I will leave and you can have your English sponsor and all the other fools sending you money.'

Lee didn't know what to do. He couldn't believe what he was hearing. And he couldn't believe Ning's casual answer to the German's question. It was all too much for him. So Lee sprung out of his chair and lunged at Tomas. Tomas stepped back quickly. Lee raised his fists but Tomas waved him away.

Tomas: 'No, that won't get you anywhere. Besides, there is something you need to see.'

Lee, fuming: 'I'll see you out cold on the floor, you fucking twat.'

Within moments the bar staff, Thai waitress's and a couple of Thai men, grabbed Lee the aggressor and shoved him out of the bar into the street. Lee was shouting and swearing at everyone in sight. This left Tomas to twist the knife on Ning.

Tomas, approaching Ning who was still sitting calmly, unperturbed: 'You know what I have, Ning?' He grinned and then pulled out his smartphone, scrolled through some pictures and thrust the phone towards Ning. 'Remember these photos, Ning? There you are, Ning, showing your tight little pussy for me, and your nice little titties.' Ning's face showed horror all of a sudden. Tomas grinned and scrolled his phone more. 'And videos of you, Ning. Yes, remember the videos of you sucking my cock? I have them all here. Very nice, Ning. You are a real professional lady.'

Ning put her hands to her face and her mouth fell open.

Tomas, ginning maliciously: 'You know what I'm going to do, Ning? I'm going to send these pictures to your family. I have your mother's number. And I'm sure your family in Isaan will love to see what their darling little girl does for a living.'

Ning: 'Oh, no…oh, nooooo…'

Tomas, putting his smartphone away: 'The choice is yours, my dear. You know my account number. I want five hundred thousand baht by tomorrow or your family will see the most charming photos of their sweet little girl in action.'

JACK AND MINNIE

There is a well known word for a farang who falls for a bar girl. It's called a Simp. Jack knew if he proceeded with his relationship with Minnie then he would eventually be called a simp. In fact, that's exactly what he and Kenny thought of Lee. It didn't take a genius to figure out that Ning was treating Lee like a simp. And now Lee was talking about marrying the girl. Crazy. But was Jack doing the same thing, going to fall down the same hole?

Jack liked Minnie. He liked her last year, especially when they went to the island together. Koh Samet. What a lovely island, and Minnie was the perfect girl to be with. It was a magical time. But then, when they returned to Pattaya, it had all gone pear shaped. They were spending time together but Jack got paranoid about Minnie's constant use of her mobile phone. It seemed to increase daily. Every night out, Minnie was texting people and receiving texts, and going out of the noisy bar to talk to someone on her mobile phone. Yes, Jack got paranoid and it caused them to fall out.

But he still couldn't help but feel Minnie was genuine. Not like a lot of the other avaricious Thai girls you hear about. Minnie was real. She needed someone to look after her. And when Jack had seen her touting for business along Beach Road late at night...well, that broke Jack's heart. Is that what she had become? Maybe she started out like that. All he knew is that he wanted to look after Minnie.

So Jack and Minnie were out on the town together. They were in a bar close to Walking Street. They'd had a good night.and were both in good spirits. They were having a late night dinner in a cafe when Minnie said: 'Jack, when you come see my family?'

Jack, thinking he hadn't heard this in a while: 'When do you want me to see them?'

Minnie: 'Anytime you want. I tell them you stay at their house in Isaan.'

Jack: 'I don't have long left for my holiday, Minnie. I'm booked to stay here in Pattaya.'

Minnie: 'But you said you would come visit them.'

Jack: 'That was last year, Minnie, I said that. We haven't seen each other since then.'

Jack wasn't sure what to do with this relationship, if that's what you could call it. He still had no idea what the future was. He didn't trust anyone and couldn't say Minnie was any different. He just didn't want to see her walking Beach Road at night again.

Jack looked once again into Minnie's beautiful face. He held her hand and kissed her. 'Minnie, when the time is right, I'll come and visit your family. Promise.'

Minnie smiled and hugged Jack, who so much wanted to be sincere, but felt life just wasn't that easy. Trusting people is something he still couldn't get used to.

JACK, KENNY, JOEY AND VINNIE

Joey, sitting down at the beachfront bar complex they were so used to by now: 'Have you seen Pete?'

Kenny, ordering the beers from the Thai waitress: 'No. Last time was here.'

Joey: 'Looks like he's gone AWOL. Him and Billy have disappeared. I've checked at the hotel. The receptionist said they took off quickly. Don't know where.'

Kenny, grinning: 'They haven't run off to get married have they?'

Vinnie, grinning: 'I was starting to think the same thing about those two.'

Jack: 'No, I think they are up to something.'

The drinks were served and all eyes were on Jack.

Joey: 'What makes you think they are up to something?'

Jack, wondering for a moment how he could explain his anxiety: "When we were here the other day, Billy said to Pete something about, 'should we tell them, Pete'. Well, what I want to know is, 'tell us what'.

The others looked at each other, then they all laughed.

Joey: 'So it's true: they are an item!'

Kenny, laughing but shaking his head: 'Nooo, can't be. I've never seen anything like that in Pete. He likes the girls.'

Vinnie: 'Come on, Kenny, they were in a loony bin together. If that's not enough to change people.'

Kenny, shrugging: 'Suppose so. Must admit, it's a bit of a strange friendship.'

Jack, shaking his head: 'No, I don't think it's that. I think it's something a bit more sinister than that.'

They all looked at Jack. Then Joey said, 'Okay, Sherlock, let's have your brilliant deduction.'

Jack, looking at Kenny: 'Kenny, you mentioned that Dutch bloke and Billy acted as if he knew all about him.'

Kenny, shrugging: 'Well, Pete's told him all about that. So what?'

Jack: 'But when you mentioned the Dutchman I noticed Billy acted strangely. I think he said something to you like, 'What do you know about the Dutchman?' Like as if he was…well, wanted to know any info on him.'

Vinnie: 'So? Do you think they are planning something?'

Jack: 'Exactly. Do you know where this Dutch fella might be now, Vinnie?'

Vinnie: 'Well, he was in Jomtien but that was last year. Don't know about now.'

Joey, to Jack: 'So what are you suggesting? Should we find the Dutchman and warn him about an oncoming attack?'

Kenny: 'Fuck that! I bottled that Dutch cunt and I'd fucking do it again. Jesus, what would have happened to Pete if we hadn't rescued him?'

Jack: 'This is what I mean. That Dutchman kidnapped Pete, drugged him and put him on stage in that weirdo place. What that Dutch cunt did was evil, he's probably done it to loads of others and he could be involved in Snuff movies and Christ knows what else.'

Vinnie: 'So what are you suggesting?'

Jack: 'I'm just saying that's probably the reason Pete has brought his psycho mate Billy out here to Pattaya. I reckon they are hunting him down. What he did to Pete was unforgivable, and they are now planning revenge. When Billy said, 'shall we tell them'?, I think that's it. I think they've got a plan going. And it probably involves murder.'

JACK AND KENNY

It was late at night and Jack and Kenny hadn't bothered going out. Sometimes in Pattaya you need a night away from the booze and the birds. So Jack was in Kenny's hotel room watching TV. Thai TV. A news programme with subtitles in English.

Jack: 'Tasty bird. There's something about Thai people, even when they're presenting a news programme, they always look like they're having a laugh.'

Kenny: 'I'd bar fine her any day.'

Jack: 'Me, too. She's a bit saucy as well. I love that cheeky smile of hers.'

So they had a few cans together. With Joey and Vinnie shagging that Brummy bird and Pete and Billy going underground, it was nice to have a quiet night in. Then Jack said, 'Switch your laptop on, Kenny. I want to search for something.'

Kenny: 'What?'

Jack: 'I want to search for that Dutch fella. You never know what might pop up on the internet.'

Kenny, grimacing: 'You're not still on about that, are you?'

Jack: 'Won't do any harm. Just let's have a look. There could be something interesting.'

Kenny switched his laptop on and they sat together going through it.

Kenny: 'What are we searching for, exactly?'

Jack, shrugging: 'Not sure where to start. How about bar owners, Pattaya?'

Kenny: 'Okay.' He typed in bar owners Pattaya into Google. It came up with all kinds of colourful stuff, lots of girls in skimpy clothes, lots of cheesy farang faces promoting their bars. But not what they were looking for.

Jack: 'Okay, try Sado Masochistic clubs, Pattaya.'

Kenny grimaced before typing into Google: 'Sado Mask…Sad Masko…How do you spell..?'

Jack, remembering spelling was not Kenny's strong point: 'Just type in SM clubs, Pattaya.'

Kenny typed in SM Clubs Pattaya. They screen threw up all kinds of weird stuff, but no more weird than what they'd seen in that club last year.

Kenny: 'So what are we looking for?' They scanned the screen. Not much of interest.

Jack: 'Okay, how about a more specific search. How about…..SM club brawl causes it to close suddenly.'

Kenny: 'What? SM club brawl…'

Jack repeated it and the screen threw up a lot more info. And some of it was really interesting. They started seeing posts like, 'SM club closed', 'Pattaya SM shut down amid controversy'. Then it got better.

Jack: 'Click on that one, there, Kenny. The one that says, 'Was Pattaya SM club a front for sex trafficking?'

Kenny clicked on the post from six months ago. And what the screen threw up was most interesting. Jack and Kenny scanned the screen, read the news report and looked at the photos of weirdos in kinky black gear. And one photo was most interesting.

Jack, gritting his teeth: 'There he is. There's that fucking Dog cunt there.'

They both glared at the screen. There was a grinning photo of that Dutchman, Michael Van Langren, and a caption that read: SM Club owner denies he was involved in illegal pornography and trafficking.

Jack and Kenny read the comments underneath the Dutchman's photo. And what alarming reading it made. The beauty of the internet is that it is out there, and if you have committed any heinous crimes then the people are out there as well. The ones who want to call you out for those crimes. And the crimes of Dutch Michael were well and truly being called out here. Comments claiming he was on the run from Interpol, had been imprisoned in Netherlands for making child pornography, then released on a balmy technicality, had embezzled money from a company he partly owned, had operated internet scams. The comments went on and on and got more and more ruthless.

Jack shook his head in disgust: 'Well, well, what a fucking charming character this is.'

Kenny, grinning: 'I'm proud to say I knocked him out with a

bottle of champagne.'

Jack: 'Should have cut his fucking throat with it.'

Kenny: 'So you think that's what Billy and Pete are planning to do?'

Jack nodded: 'Yes. I mean, they will have seen this on the internet.'

Kenny: 'You reckon so?'

Jack: 'Absolutely. I mean, the thing about these psychos, they are very intelligent. They're probably far more up to date on the internet and stuff than we are. Those of us who have day jobs. And you said something about Pete and Billy being a strange friendship, didn't you?'

Kenny, nodding: 'Does seem a bit weird. I mean, Billy's a big hard bastard while Pete's, well, he can have a go but only if he's got support. He's not hard by himself.'

Jack: 'But don't you see, that's not so unusual for a Psycho friendship. You will often find a strong personality befriends a weaker one. That way the strong one can tell his sidekick what to do. A psycho probably likes having a timid friend who he can manipulate. Just think about it. Charles Manson had control over an army of misfits, mostly young girls. He could manipulate them. They even committed murders for him.'

Kenny looked back at the photo of the shady Dutchman. 'So you think they are targeting him? So what are we gonna do?'

Jack: 'I don't know. I just don't know. I'd like to see that Dutch cunt dead, but don't forget, it's your mate who is gonna be involved in it. I don't give a damn about Pete anymore, he's proved to be a complete owlarse. It's up to you, Kenny. You're the one who's grown up with him.'

Kenny shrugged: 'Fuck knows. So long as they don't try to drag us into it.'

LEE AT A BAR, ALONE

'You like lady?' the Thai girl said to the man sitting at the bar. The man at the bar didn't answer. Just sat silently, morbidly, hunched over the bar like a drunk about to collapse. He was drinking another Thai whiskey. It was after ten in the evening and he didn't know how many he'd had that day. Started drinking early in the day, kept going, drinking alone. The Thai girl prodded him to get his attention. 'You like lady?' she said again.

Lee, angrily: 'NO! No I don't fucking like lady! I just want to be left alone!'

The Thai girl stepped back in alarm, and left the man alone at the bar.

Lee was depressed. He was angry. He felt humiliated, taken for a mug yet again. At first his anger was toward that German twat. Lee wished he hadn't hesitated, just got up and knocked out the bastard. But then….he thought. Was it the German who had taken him for a mug? Lied to him, cheated on him? No, it was Ning who did that.

Lee held up his glass to the Thai girl behind the bar. She brought him another Thai whiskey. Lee drank, wondering what to do next. He'd had all day to think, and he'd decided he didn't want to see Ning again. What disturbed him was how casual she was about it all. He pays more money than you, she had said to the German. So that was it, was it? That was all he meant to her? More money than the next guy. So how many more other guys, mugs, were there who were sending her money each month? And were they all shagging her as well? Of course they were. The thought of it made Lee's blood boil. How could she? Beautiful Ning, his Thai girl who he wanted to bring to England and marry. How could she do this, so coldly, heartlessly?

Lee downed his whiskey and slammed the glass down on the bar, causing alarm from the bar staff. 'You okay?' one of the bar girls said. Lee didn't answer. He didn't want to act like an aggressive drunk but a guy can only take so much. What could he do now? Just what could he do now? He needed to talk. He needed the company of a friend right now.

Lee took out his smartphone and searched for Kenny's number. Lee liked those Scouse fellas and had made friends with them.

Right now, he needed a friend to talk to. He dialled Kenny's number.

It was half an hour later when Jack and Kenny entered the bar. Lee couldn't remember what he had said to Kenny over the phone, but they both looked concerned as they approached Lee at the bar.

Kenny, taking a seat and ordering drinks for the three men: 'You okay, Lee? Everything alright?'

Lee was drunk. He looked at Kenny, then turned to Jack. 'No. Not okay. It's all...fucking...all...'

Kenny looked at Jack knowingly. Lee had had a few too many. But, even so, they were taken aback when Lee slumped his head on the bar and started crying. Jack looked at Kenny and shrugged. Kenny did the same. This was worse than they thought.

It probably wasn't as unusual to see a forty something man cry as you may think. Men cry for all kinds of reasons. Losing at the casino, England losing at a World Cup, and women. Yes, men cry over women. It seemed Lee was crying over a Thai freelancer. Jack and Kenny just didn't know what to make of this.

Lee, blubbing: 'She's been cheating on me. She's cheated on me.'

Kenny, not surprised: 'Ning? Well, Lee, are you really surprised?'

Lee, drunkenly turning to Kenny: 'What's that supposed...? I don't know. I just don't know. I'm... fucking...sick.'

Jack: 'So what happened exactly?'

Lee: 'I was with her in a bar and some German twat came up and caused a scene. He said he'd been sending her money and... he wanted the money back...She's been shagging him. And she's been shagging fuck knows how many other...'

Kenny, shrugging: 'Lee, you should know by now, these girls are out there to make money. That's all they think about.'

Lee: 'But I feel so foolish. I'm stupid. I feel like a mug. I thought we had something.' He banged his fist on the bar. 'I fucking hate women. I hate them. I was ripped off by my wife, she took everything and I…I'm just sick of being taken for a mug.'

Jack: 'Well, Lee, you know what you have to do first. Stop sending her money. I don't want to sound cruel, but I can understand that German guy wanting his money back.'

Lee, alarmed: 'What? What ya mean, you understand that twat?'

Jack: 'I mean…awww, I dunno. Look, forget about him. Just think of yourself. You've been hurt and cheated and hopefully you'll learn a lesson.' It flashed through Jack's mind what he was going to do about Minnie. He'd think about that later.

Kenny, ordering another round of drinks: 'Look, Lee, you're a decent bloke and you've been hurt, but it's not the end of the world. You are in a place where there are plenty more birds around. And remember, at least you've got friends. You can hang around with us for the rest of the time here, no problem. Something Our Kid (Kenny's older brother) once said to me, 'Never fight with your mates over women. Coz good mates are hard to come by. Women are ten a penny.' Always remember that.'

Lee looked at Kenny through tearful eyes. Then he looked at Jack and said, 'You're a good pair of lads, you are. A good pair of lads.'

JACK SCANNING THE INTERNET

Jack woke the next morning, alone in bed, wishing Minnie was next to him. He'd told her he needed a quiet night with his friends and she understood. He couldn't fault Minnie right now. It was like as if she'd learned her lesson. That lesson involving mobile phones and constant texting and stuff. Now, whenever she and Jack were together, it was a better relationship. And Jack had to admit, in spite of all the warnings he had heard about never trusting a bar girl, he had become besotted with Minnie once again.

But, for now, there was another issue that needed clearing up.

Jack got out of bed and put the kettle on. Coffee to start the day. It was 10.30 and no one had anything planned today. He'd phone Minnie later and arrange to meet her.

Jack switched his laptop on and began scanning Youtube. He checked out the channel with the Australian guy reading news reports. There was still no more word on the condition of the guy who was in hospital. Maybe no news is good news. But it seemed strange that the others seemed oblivious to it. Jack seemed to be the only one worried that they may get an unexpected knock at the door. Hopefully there was no CCTV in that bar. They would be wise to avoid that Soi Buakhao area, that's for sure.

So Jack continued to scan Youtube, watched videos on Pattaya, what's going on, reviews, anything that could be useful. He typed in 'Pattaya vlogs' and a list of videos came up. Some of these vloggers he was now used to. Watching a Thai based Youtuber while sat at home in Liverpool on Winter's night was something Jack found irresistible.

Jack flicked through the list of food reviews, nightlife reviews, youtubers giving advice on healthcare, visas, all kinds of stuff. And one of the Youtubers he'd watched before was Lenny Pazazz. This was a guy with quite big production values, a bar owner who seemed to employ a lot of people. He made a few videos with his team and was quite entertaining. And he did a rather good weekly live show on Friday nights, with bar girls, live music, all kinds of cheesy stuff. Jack liked him, but he did get a lot of trolls who found his 'Seventies DJ' persona to be a bit over the top.

So Jack watched a replay of Lenny Pazazz's recent livestream. The streams took place in his crowded bar and was just the kind of braindead entertainment you could fall into either very late at night or first thing in the morning. Jack was drinking his third cup of coffee, watching Lenny Pazazz parading around the bar interviewing people, all of them farangs who'd already had a few beers. And then Lenny stopped to talk to another customer. A customer who Jack had seen before. And then, when the customer opened his mouth and began talking, with that sly, smug grin on his face, Jack realised who it was.

Jack shook his head. It was all coming together now. This was the final piece of the jigsaw. 'Ohhhhh, fuck..... So that's where they are targeting.'

JACK TELLS KENNY WHAT HE'S FOUND

Kenny, watching the replay of the Lenny Pazazz show on his laptop: 'Jesus, who does this guy think he is? Lenny Pazazz. What kind of stupid name is that? Looks like an old Seventies DJ. Just look at his teeth. That poncey hairdo. I'm surprised he isn't wearing a shiny suit.'

Jack: 'He's a bit of a character. I know he's as cheesy as fuck but he puts a good show together. I often watch it late at night. Just the kind of braindead entertainment you can watch before going to bed."

Kenny: 'Well, I still think he's a knobhead. Anyway, what's this you want to show me?'

Jack: 'Just fast forward the video. Keep going. Bit further. There, we're coming up to it now. Stop. Now play it from here.'

Kenny pressed the play button and watched as Lenny Pazazz was interviewing customers in his bar. It wasn't long before he saw what Jack wanted him to see. Kenny grimaced: 'There's that fucking cunt.'

Jack: 'Keep listening, Kenny. This is the important point coming up.'

They watched the replay with Lenny Pazazz telling his viewers that Michael, this Dutch charmer who was opening a Ladyboy club, would be appearing with some of his ladyboys on his show on Friday night. Live on the Lenny Pazazz Youtube show.

Jack and Kenny sat before the laptop, thinking their own thoughts, what they could make of this.

Kenny, turning to Jack: 'So? What do you reckon?'

Jack: 'I reckon that's where the Terrible Twins are going to be targeting. That's where the Dutchman's going to be. We know where he is, what time he'll be there and it's going to be broadcast live on YouTube.'

Kenny: 'But what makes you think Pete and Billy have seen this?'

Jack: 'It's a hunch I have. I know for a fact that Pete watches Youtube. He was around at my pad one night when I was watching some of these Thailand vloggers and I think he's got hooked on it as well. I know he watches this stuff. He will have seen this. And it's going to be live, so that Dutchman is gonna be there at that time. I just get the feeling, wherever Pete and Billy are, they are planning an attack. And it could even happen right there, in that bar. Tonight.'

CHAPTER ELEVEN

THERE'S NOTHING I LIKE BETTER THAN A GOOD MURDER

There is an area away from Pattaya centre called The Darkside. It's an area where a lot of expats live. It got its name because of its lack of street lighting. It's an area with bars, cheaper beer, a cheaper cost of accommodation. It's here that Pete and Billy had suddenly moved to get away from any disruptions that may occur. They had moved into a small condo, a nice place away from everything. Away from any questions.

Billy stood in front of the mirror, swooshing his machete about. It was Friday morning, and he and Pete were making the final rehearsals for the big show tonight. They had everything sorted. It was going to be a perfectly executed plan. No hiccups.

Billy, swooshing the machete about: 'Are you feeling good today, Pete?'

Pete, sitting on the bed watching Lenny Pazazz on Youtube: 'Sorted.'

Billy, grinning: 'That's good to hear, Pete. You know, Pete, I am so glad we met each other. We are a perfect partnership. A team of two. Two's enough. We really don't need any others.'

Pete, nodding: 'I don't want any others. This is our day, it's all about us.'

Billy: 'That's the spirit, Pete. That's the spirit.'

Billy continued swooshing the machete about in perfect motion, handling it lovingly. He stopped and got closer to the mirror. He grinned at his own reflection. He was looking at a face which would eventually be recognised across the world. A face that would become an iconic image like that of Manson or the Krays. A face that would adorn book covers, documentaries, magazines and videos.

Billy smiled: 'This is your day, Billy,' he said to his reflection. 'This is the day that you get famous.' Then Billy's face cracked into a malicious smile and he said, 'There's nothing I like better than a good murder.'

THE LADS

Joey: 'Lenny who? Never fucking heard of him.'
Jack: 'He does a Youtube show. He's doing a livestream at his bar tonight. And that Dutch cunt is going to be there with his ladyboys.'

They were all sitting at their usual bar on Beach Road. It was Friday afternoon.

Vinnie: 'So you reckon Pete and Billy are going to storm in there and cause murder?'

Jack: 'Pete's unbalanced. He's got every reason to want revenge on that Dutchman, and Billy is the perfect psycho who is going to help him.'

Joey: 'But what are they going to do? Go in there like Arnold, start blasting, Hasta La Vista, Baby?'

Jack: 'Wouldn't surprise me. All I know is that it's going to be live and that Dutchman's gonna be there tonight.'

Kenny: 'I still can't see how they're gonna do him in front of so many witnesses.'

Jack: 'Do you think they care? They're both off their rocker, and that Billy, he's a real Basket Case. For all we know they could be wearing masks.'

Joey laughed: 'This gets more and more Sherlock Holmes by the minute. Are you sure you haven't been watching too many old movies, Jack?'

Jack: 'You can laugh. But isn't Pete supposed to be your mate, Joey? I just thought you may be concerned for him. I mean, they've both gone underground, haven't they? Don't you think there's a reason for that?'

Vinnie had a sudden strange look on his face. He turned to Jack. 'What was that you said a minute ago? Basket Case?'

Jack, nodding; 'It's a casual term for a psycho. Used in movies, that sort of thing.'

Vinnie sat back in alarm and said, 'That's it! That's where I've seen him before. Basket Case Billy.'

They all looked at Vinnie.

Vinnie: 'Don't you remember some years ago, Basket Case Billy was in the news. Made national headlines. Guy was a well known psychotic around, I think it was the Dingle area, and he murdered someone, can't remember who, but it was in a pub. And the fucker got off with it! Plenty of witnesses but they were all too terrified to speak up. Guy was a real nutter. That's what they called him behind his back. Basket Case Billy.' Vinnie looked at the numb faces of Jack, Kenny and Joey. 'It's him. I remember his picture in the papers. It's definitely him.'

Jack, Kenny and Joey all looked at each other. This was going from bad to worse. And then Kenny called the waitress over and said, 'I think we all need another drink.'

CAROL AND LIZZY BY THE POOL

Lizzy: 'Are you still shagging those two Scousers?'
Carol, opening her eyes: 'Yes, they're a pair of corkers, they are.'
It was Friday afternoon and Carol and Lizzy were lying on the sunbeds beside the hotel pool. George and Jeff had disappeared again. It seemed to be a regular thing. The men disappearing and Lizzy and Carol lying by the pool every day. This is some holiday, Lizzy thought.

Lizzy: 'It's turned out good for you here, hasn't it? I mean, you're having a threesome with them two, George and Jeff are disappearing everyday, probably to some Thai brothel and I'm left here satisfying my sweaty minge without so much as a vibrator for company.'

Carol grinned: 'Oh, don't worry. Your time will come. You'll be back in Gambia next year shagging all kinds. I'm coming with you as well. Okay, so I've touched lucky here, but things are gonna be different next time.'

Lizzy: 'How are things gonna be different? I reckon George and Jeff are gettin their fill here so they'll want to come back again and again. I swear it, If I catch that husband of mine shagging any of these Thial prostitutes I'll fucking strangle him.'

Carol, sitting up and rubbing her eyes: 'So that's where you think they're going everyday?'

Lizzy: 'Course it is. I'm not fucking stupid. It's written all over their faces. And I'm sure George smells different.'

Carol: 'Smells different? How?'

Lizzy: 'I mean cleaner. Like he's showering somewhere. He usually comes home sweaty but now it's like he's just come out of a shower.'

Carol, laughing: 'For fuck's sake, Lizzy...'

Lizzy: 'What are you laughing at?'

Carol: 'I mean, the thought of your George getting his dick washed in the shower by one of those little Thai girls!' Carol then went into a fit of uncontrollable laughter, which only made Lizzy more annoyed.

Lizzy: 'You can laugh, but Jeff is probably doing the same thing. I just don't trust them two.'

Carol: 'I don't give a shite what Jeff gets up to anymore. He does nothing for me. So long as I can get the house I don't care.'

Lizzy: 'So what happens then? Do you carry on shagging those two Scousers? I wouldn't trust that pair.'

Carol: 'Fuck, lighten up, Lizzy. Lighten up.'

JACK AND MINNIE

Jack and Minnie spent the afternoon together. They visited the Sanctuary Of Truth, a marvellous, huge wooden temple in the Na Klua area of Pattaya. When you see this temple from Wongamat beach it looks majestic, and is no less so when you step inside the place.

Jack, entering the temple with Minnie: 'Wow, this place is awesome.' He thought for a moment that his own city of Liverpool had itself some truly amazing buildings, especially the two cathedrals. But this place had the true wow factor. Some say in Asia, 'you've seen one temple, you've seen them all', but that's not true. The Sanctuary of Truth, still being built after so many years, is a marvellous structure of intricate carvings and religious symbolism. Just being in a place like this felt quite special. And, to have the company of Minnie felt so good. She was the perfect companion, Jack thought.

Minnie, sensing Jack's enthusiasm for this place: 'You like it here, Jack?'

Jack: 'Yes, it's amazing.' He smiled at her. 'And all the better for being with you.'

After touring the temple, they stopped at a nearby cafe and had coffee and cakes. It was a lovely afternoon, and as Jack sat at this roadside cafe in a charming area with Minnie, he felt that rare moment when he just wanted time to stop. He wanted this moment to last forever.

So what was Jack going to do? He was faced with the choice that many men were faced with when they met and fell for a Thai girl. There was something called the Three Day Rule. This means if you hook up with a bar girl, don't be with her for more than three days otherwise the relationship turns into something it shouldn't and before you know it she'll be telling you the sob story of the sick buffalo at her parents farm in Isaan. Well, whatever the three day rule was, Jack had already crossed that line. And now, as his holiday was drawing to a close, he was left with the terrible decision of what to do with Minnie.

Just what could he do? He had already decided he wasn't going to be one of those mugs who send the girls money, only for them to carry on working. Just look at Lee. Poor guy breaking down in tears after being used for so long. So what could Jack do? Just say, thanks for a good time, Minnie, and then go home leaving her to carry on plying her trade on Beach Road. There were no easy answers. He wasn't heartless, but he was no mug, either. So he'd need to think very carefully about it.

Don't be heartless. Don't be a mug. Be realistic.

KENNY, JOEY AND VINNIE

Kenny, Joey and Vinnie were in the Beer Garden having dinner. Jack and Minnie were somewhere together, Billy and Pete had gone AWOL.

The Beer Garden is one of Pattaya's old stalwarts, a beachfront wooden restaurant with great food, drink and fabulous views over Pattaya.

So the three were having their beers while looking out over the sea. It was around 3pm. Time to order some food, have a couple more drinks then head back to the hotel for a bit of rest before a night on the town. But they all had things on their mind. It was Jack who had filled their heads with the thought of Billy, Pete and that Lenny Pazazz show. And no one had decided what to do yet.

Kenny: 'Do you think Jack's right about that thing tonight?'

Vinnie, pawing through the menu: 'Fuck knows.'

Joey: 'I think Jack's been watching too much Sherlock Holmes.'

Kenny, looking out at the boats: 'I dunno, it seems to make sense to me.'

Joey: 'So what's gonna happen?'

Vinnie: 'Whatever's gonna happen it hasn't happened yet, so don't worry about it.'

Kenny: 'Yes, but we need to think about it. I mean, if Pete ends up in a Thai prison then his family are gonna say it's our fault. They'll say we should have done more to stop him doing whatever he's doing.'

Joey: 'What? His family don't give a fuck about him anymore. That's why he ended up in a fucking loony bin with that other psycho. Nah, I wouldn't worry about it.'

Kenny: 'But I still reckon we should be at that place. You never know, he may need us.'

Vinnie: 'So in other words we should go to this poxy show at a poxy bar to see if Pete and Billy show up and do something we don't even know if they have planned yet? Sounds a bit bizarre.'

Kenny: 'Vinnie, haven't you forgotten something? You know that Dutch guy better than the rest of us. For all we know there could be more to it. And Pete has a bad grudge against him. I don't blame him. And that Dutch fella is going to be there at that time. I'm starting to think Jack's right. I reckon they're gonna target him tonight.'

Joey: 'Okay, if it keeps you and Sherlock happy, we'll go there tonight. Just to see if them two show up. But I'm not hanging around if it's full of fucking ladyboys.'

They had their dinner at the Beer Garden before heading back to their hotels for a late afternoon kip. The Lenny Pazazz show was just hours away.

LENNY PAZAZZ

Lenny entered the bar at 7pm. The show was beginning at 9pm, so it gave him two hours to check everything before going live. He was greeted by the girls in the bar, not many customers yet.

It was going to be a lively show. They had Tommy Wallis, with his piano and Liberace tribute act, as well as a featured ladyboy show. Lenny was going to interview Micheal, the owner of the new ladyboy club. Lenny still didn't feel comfortable with that, and wished they'd never agreed to have him on the show. No less that four bar owners had spoken to him this last week and mentioned the rumours about the Dutchman's shady past. But what the hell, Pattaya was full of shady characters so that's nothing new. And it was too late to have a change of plan now. At least the ladyboy show would be good, so that's all that mattered.

Lenny, to Seamus, his sidekick: 'Alright, Seamus. Everything looking good?'

Seamus, testing the cameras and microphones: 'All good. It's gonna be a good show.'

Lenny was pleased to hear it. He went to the bar and ordered himself a pot of tea before going online and checking his Youtube channel. He was up to 76,000 subscribers. Not in the big league of Youtubers, but he was doing well. His Friday night livestream could reach thousands of viewers across the globe and was the perfect platform for promoting his bar. Not a stairway to the stars, but he was doing well. And tonight was going to be a really good show. He had a good feeling about it.

KENNY VISITS JACK

Jack and Minnie returned to the hotel and went to the room. The plan was to have a few hours sleep and then go out on the town together. But Kenny had other ideas.

It was after seven pm when Kenny knocked on Jack's door. Jack was in bed with Minnie and was annoyed at being disturbed. He went to the door and opened it.

Kenny: 'We're going to the bar, Jack. All of us. Let's get a taxi at 8.30. The show starts at 9.'

Jack, feeling drowsy: 'What? Oh, I dunno. I got to think about that. I'm with Minnie.'

Kenny, looking surprised: 'Come on, Jack. You can't change your mind now. You were the one who put us on to all this. Joey and Vinnie are coming.'

Jack, shaking his head sleepily: 'I dunno. I've been thinking. Why should I care about Pete? He's never liked me any more than I've liked him. He's shown his true colours. Whatever he gets up to with that nutter, well, as long as we're not involved.'

Kenny, vociferous: 'But we are involved, Jack. There's still someone on a life support machine that we may all face charges over. If them two get up to something bad then we may get accused of planning it all. Look, let's just get there and see what happens.'

Jack, rolling his eyes: 'Ohhhh, shite. Okay, then, I'll be ready for 8.30. But I'm bringing Minnie with me.'

Kenny: 'See you at eight thirty.'

CAROL, JOEY AND VINNIE

Carol, snuggling in bed between Joey and Vinnie: 'Fucking hell, you two fellas have really turned this holiday around for me. What a pair of cherubs you both are.'

Vinnie, rubbing Carol's fanny: 'Cherub? I've been called some things in my time but never that.'

Joey, rubbing Carol's tits: 'I'm happy to be Carol's cherub. So long as I can get my rocks off, I'm happy.'

Carol, laughing and grabbing both of their dicks: 'Who'd have thought? This holiday was shit before you two came along. And now I'm having the time of my life.'

Joey: 'How's your mate doing? Big whatshername.'

Carol: 'Lizzy. And don't ever call her Big Lizzy. She's touchy about that. Yes, she's a bit miserable, but she's still got that little wimp of a husband.'

Vinnie: 'How about your husband? What's he doing?'

Carol: 'Oh, him? I don't fucking care anymore, he's just a twat.'

Joey: 'So what are you going to do? Divorce him.'

Carol: 'Probably. So long as I get the house, I don't care.'

Joey, liking the sound of that: 'So if you get the house you can sell it and come and live out here.'

Vinnie, also liking the sound of that: 'Yes, and you've got a couple of cherubs for company, don't forget.'

Carol: 'Sounds like a wonderful idea.'

Vinnie's phone rang and he picked it up. It was Kenny. 'Okay, Vinnie. Me and Jack and his missus are going to that bar. The show starts at 9pm. Meet us there.'

Vinnie: 'Okay.' He hung up.

Carol: 'Who was that?'

Vinnie: 'Kenny, our mate. We're all going to some bar tonight. We reckon there's gonna be a big argy bargy going on there and we want to see it.'

Carol: 'What? A fight?'

Joey: 'Something like that.'

Carol: 'Well, if that's the case, I'm coming with you. I could do with a bit of excitement tonight.'

Vinnie: 'Okay, you come with us. I'll phone a taxi for 8.30.'

Carol, hesitating: 'Er, is it okay if I bring Lizzy with us? She's down in the dumps and needs a bit of cheering up.'

Joey, looking at Vinnie: 'What? Big...I mean, your mate? She's not going to like it if I'm there.'

Carol: 'Oh, behave yourself. She's got nothing against you. She's a woman of the world. She just needs cheering up, that's all. You just be polite to her.'

Vinnie grinned: 'I know. And, remember, Joey, whatever you do, don't call her Big Lizzy.'

JACK, KENNY AND MINNIE

The bar was in Soi 13, a Soi between Second Road and Beach Road. There were plenty of girly bars around, loud music pumping out everywhere. There were not so many cries of, 'Hello, sexy man,' when Kenny, Jack and Minnie stepped out of the Bolt taxi. Maybe it was Minnie's presence that held them back.

Kenny, walking down the bustling Soi with Jack and Minnie: 'Never seen this area before. Pattaya is huge. Just when you think you've seen it all, something like this pops up.'

Jack nodded: 'Yes, it's a fair size.'

They walked a hundred metres down the dark Soi. The thumping techno music was loud, but then gave way to a much more gentle sound. Piano music. They walked a few paces more and the piano music got louder, more raunchy. Then they could hear a man singing, Las Vegas cabaret style. 'Hello,' a busty Thai girl called from outside a bar. 'You come inside. We have show tonight.'

They stopped outside the bar. It looked more impressive than the other places. It had a doorway with a security man outside, and bright lights with the sign, 'LENNYS' above the door.

Jack looked at Kenny: 'This is the one.'

It was rocking inside. Lots of people, Thai girls, farangs, and the piano player was really getting the crowd going.

Kenny, observing the piano player: 'Fuck me, it's Liberace.'

Jack: 'I did read that they had a Liberace tribute act tonight.'

Kenny: 'Liberace. Ladyboys. I hope it's not one of those places.'

Jack: 'Nah, don't worry about it. They'll leave you alone if you're not interested.'

Kenny: 'It's okay for you, you're with Minnie. It's me they'll be harassing.'

Jack, always fearing Kenny's moods when he's in a place he doesn't like: 'No one is going to harass you. Now let's get some drinks.'

Jack, Kenny and Minnie found a nice little table near the corner and were served their drinks. Jack liked having Minnie with him coz it kept the bar girls away. Kenny was approached by a couple of girls but didn't seem interested. He was in one of his grumpy moods. Thing about Kenny, if he liked a place he would let you know about it. Unfortunately, if he didn't like a place he would also let you know about that. And his irascible temper could often be alarming. Jack hoped he wouldn't kick off. This night had enough questions over it without having to deal with his best mate.

It sure was a rocking bar. A big enough place, and the crowds were starting to pour in. Lenny Pazazz, the popular Youtuber and owner of the bar, was visible over the other side. He and his sidekick, Seamus, were sitting with headphones on while a bunch of raunchy Thai girls were dancing around Liberace, with his red velvet suit and permed hair.

Jack, swigging his beer: 'Hey, Kenny. He's good.'

Kenny, frowning: 'Good? You mean Liberace over there. Give over.'

Jack: 'Awww, come on, it's all a bit of fun. He's got a good voice and he even looks a bit like him.'

Kenny: 'As long as none of these weirdos come near me.'

Jack took another swig of his beer, and decided Kenny could be one miserable cunt at times.

Minnie: 'You want dance, Jack?'

Jack: 'Nahh, not in the mood, Minnie. You can dance if you want to.'

Minnie, snuggling close to Jack: 'I stay with you.'

Jack: 'Okay. It's not going to be a long night here. We go somewhere else afterwards.'

Kenny: 'Here's the boys coming in. And just look what they've got with them.'

Jack looked towards the doorway to see Joey and Vinnie walking in. With two women. One was a plump blonde. The other was...oh, dear....

Kenny: 'Don't tell me that's what they've been shagging!'

Jack: 'I think they're both porking the blonde one. The other monster, fuck knows.'

Joey, beaming: 'Alright, lads. What's happening? I see Liberace is over there.'

The Thai waitress approached the table and Joey tried his usual stunt of ordering drinks and putting the bill in someone else's check bin. Typical Joey.

Carol, to Kenny: 'Are you Jack?'

Kenny, grumpy: 'I'm Kenny. That's Jack.'

Carol: 'Nice to meet you both. I love Scousers.'

So I hear, Kenny thought. You've been shagging two of them, you dirty bitch.

The waitress brought a round of drinks, still not sure who was paying for them all. But Jack had an idea that Carol was paying the way for Joey and Vinnie, cos they never had any money. As for the big one, well.....

'Lizzy', she said, stone-faced: 'The name's Lizzy.'

Jack smiled at the woman who towered over the others and was built like a Sumo wrestler. 'Nice to meet you, Lizzy.' Kenny just grunted. He was the only single bloke around right now and he hoped she didn't target him. He'd had enough of this place already.

The four men and three women watched the show for a while.

It was quite good entertainment in the bar. Liberace was a good performer, there were plenty of farang customers about, plenty of Thai girls, banging music. The Lenny Pazazz Youtube show was in full swing but you couldn't hear the two presenters. They had headphones on while a young Thai cameraman recorded them with a big, expensive looking camera. It all seemed well organised and Lenny Pazazz clearly knew what he was doing with this set up.

It wasn't such a bad night, Jack decided. Everyone seemed happy except for grumpy Kenny and out of place Lizzy. Jack noticed Lizzy was eyeing Minnie, for whatever reason. Did Lizzy fancy her? Did Lizzy pour scorn on English guys who went with Thai girls? Or did Lizzy wonder why people in this world come in all shapes and sizes?

Kenny, tensing all of a sudden: 'There he is. There's that dog cunt over there.'

Jack and the boys looked over to the far side of the bar. They could see the Dutchman, drinking a beer and briefing his ladyboys.

Jack, gritting his teeth: 'Fucking bastard. So he's got a new ladyboy club now, has he? Shady cunt.'

Kenny, grinning proudly: 'Ahh, I knocked the cunt out, remember. Put a champagne bottle over his head. Sparked him flat out.'

Vinnie looked over to Michael, realising all of a sudden that he was the one in this gang that Michael would remember. He didn't know the faces of the other masked men after their last encounter at the SM club. Vinnie turned around and hid his face, and wondered if being here was a good idea. No one was still quite sure what was going to happen.

Lenny Pazazz sat in his chair and spoke to his Youtube viewers.

Lenny: 'So, one of the most exciting new clubs in Pattaya is about to open its doors. We'll be speaking to the owner, Michael, in a few minutes, but before that let's have a good old song and dance routine from Micheal's delightful ladyboys. Queue the music.'

There followed a song and dance routine from four immaculately dressed ladyboys, to some rather jazzy music. All very stylish for those who like that sort of thing.

Kenny: 'Must admit, some of those ladyboys look better than the girls.'

Jack: 'Sure, they look good. But it's still a bloke at the end of the day.' Jack hugged Minnie. 'Gimme a real woman, anyday.'

Lizzy, looking down on Jack and Minnie: 'Is this your Thai bride, then?'

Jack looked up at Lizzy's hideous, stern face: 'What? What's that supposed to mean?'

Lizzy: 'Is it your Thai bride?'

Jack: 'IT? IT'S name is Minnie. And she's my girlfriend.'

Lizzy: 'No need to be like that. Just asking.'

Jack: 'Well, it did seem a bit sarcastic.'

Lizzy turned away from Jack. Jack turned away from Lizzy. That was the only conversation they had between them. Thankfully.

Kenny, noticing Jack's annoyance: 'She's big. Looks like a heavyweight wrestler.'

Carol, whispering to Kenny: 'She's okay. But watch your mouth when she's around. She's touchy about her size. And whatever you do, don't call her Big Lizzy.'

Kenny: 'I wouldn't call her that. I'd be too scared.'

Jack was watching the show on his smartphone. It was broadcast live on Youtube. There were over two thousand viewers. You could see the comments from viewers on the screen. Most of the comments were good natured. For now. It would be interesting, Jack thought, how the comments would look when Dutch Michael sat in the chair to be interviewed. The internet world out there had heard about this guy and his shady past. Presumably some of the viewers would, too.

The ladyboy show finished and the Dutchman sat down next to

Lenny Pazazz. They were both grinning and smiling and it was all very cheesy, with Michael promoting his ladyboy club and giving the rundown on how spectacular it was and all that jazz. And, yes, Jack did notice from his smartphone that there were some hostile comments to the Dutchman. He was obviously well known in this fraternity, for the wrong reasons. Shady bastard, Jack thought.

The waitress brought another round of drinks for all. Jack was relieved he and Kenny were sharing their own check bin, while Joey, Vinnie, Carol and Lizzy had theirs. Presumably Joey and Vinnie were milking Carol. She appeared to be the one with money. Typical.

Kenny, getting restless: 'Shall we make this our last drink here, Jack? This place is shite.'

Jack: 'Let's give it a while longer.'

Vinnie: 'I don't feel comfortable here. I don't want that Michael to recognise me.'

Joey, to Jack: 'What's this all about then, Sherlock? I thought there was gonna be some action.'

Carol: 'Yes, where's this big fight, then? I heard there's gonna be some argy bargy here, bit of excitement.'

Lizzy, stone faced and miserable: 'It's only exciting if you like ladyboys and prozzies.'

Jack, serious: 'So you want excitement, do you? Well, it's going to happen soon.'

Kenny: 'How's it gonna happen? What's gonna happen, Jack? This is crazy. Those two clowns are not coming here.'

Jack, looking soberly to the other side of the bar: 'I know they're not coming. Because they are already here.'

Everyone looked at Jack. 'What?' they all said. 'Where?'

Jack: 'Don't look now, but over the far side, behind that table with the group of blokes on it. Two guys standing by the wall with their drinks. I've been watching them for the last twenty minutes. It's them.'

And, as they all took a glance to the far side, they realised Jack was telling the truth. Two men, standing upright like Centurions, with the most absurd fake moustaches and wigs, and carrying on their backs some highly suspicious day bags. The more the guys looked over, looked behind the absurd disguises, there was no doubt about it. Pete and Billy had gatecrashed the party.

Kenny: 'So what the fuck are we gonna do?'

Jack, cool: 'I think the question is what are they gonna do?'

Vinnie: 'Fuck me, if they have gone through the trouble to wear disguises then they must have something serious planned.'

Joey, laughing: 'Gone through the trouble? For fuck's sake, you can pick that shite up at any joke shop. They look like the fucking Marx Brothers!'

Jack decided that Vinnie's comment was the most relevant one. You don't wear a disguise unless you have something serious planned. But what exactly was going to happen?

Jack: 'Let's order another round of drinks here. I don't know what they are up to, but it's something we can't just run away from.'

They ordered a round of drinks while the ladyboys were finishing their dance routine. Jack looked at the show on his smartphone. Lenny Pazazz was back on the screen.

Lenny: 'Oh, that was really fantastic. I'm sure the Glamour Boys club is going to be a real winner. And to tell us all about it, here's the man himself. It's Michael Van Langren.'

The Dutchman called Michael Van Langren sat down in the chair next to Lenny Pazazz. He put his headphones on and smiled.

Lenny beamed: 'Michael. So glad you could join us this evening. Well, those ladyboys sure are looking good. Love those fancy evening dresses they're wearing. Now when is your actual opening night for the Naughty Boys club?'

It was a very cordial chat. They could never have known that imminent danger was just metres away from them.

The waitress brought a new round of drinks to the table. The guys were all a bit edgy, glancing over to the two menacing figures over the far side of the bar. They had all noticed that Dutch Michael had taken his chair and was being interviewed by Lenny Pazazz. If something was going to happen, and they were all by now convinced something was going to happen, then it was going to happen soon. Any moment now.

Something was happening. The guys looked towards the doorway to see some commotion. At first it looked like a fight had broken out. You know that scene in a crowded bar, when you see people pushing and shoving each other, people standing out of the way for safety, people rushing about all of a sudden. And then you realise a fight has broken out. But this wasn't a fight. Not exactly. There were Thai girls moving away from the door, people standing well back from the commotion.

Kenny: 'What the fuck's going on over there?'

They all looked over to the commotion at the doorway. And then Jack glanced over to the far side to see if Pete and Billy were still standing there. No, they weren't. It was them causing the commotion at the doorway. It had started.

There were men shouting, and Thai girls screaming, people panicking and rushing out of the way. And then it became clear what was happening. Pete and Billy, no longer in disguise, were blocking the exit to the bar. They were shoving tables and chairs and more tables and chairs, all to prevent anyone from leaving. Within a minute there appeared a mountain of chairs and tables, with people moving about away from the doorway. Jack, Kenny, Vinnie and Joey stood up to see what was happening. The doorway was now blocked by a mountain of chairs and tables. And there stood Pete and Billy, wearing silk kimonos, carrying backpacks, facing the crowd. Knives in their hands.

Billy addressed the crowd: 'NO ONE MAKE ANY ATTEMPT TO GET THROUGH THAT DOOR! NO ONE TRY TO LEAVE! WE HAVE A BOMB AND WE WILL BLOW THIS PLACE TO SMITHEREENS IF

ANYONE TRIES TO LEAVE!'

There were screams from the Thai girls. Then Pete held up the bomb in his hand. It was the size of a brick, wrapped in a cloth bag.

Kenny: 'Oh, fuck….Oh, fuck…'
Joey: 'Is this what it's come to?'
Vinnie: 'Fucking hell, fucking hell…'
Carol: 'Fucking hell, when you said there was gonna be excitement I never thought this!'
Jack: 'It's not a real bomb.'
Kenny: 'What makes you say that?'
Jack: 'Do you really think Pete's got the bottle to hold a real bomb in his hand?'
Joey: 'I dunno, he's been behaving kind of weird recently.'
Kenny: 'I think it's a real bomb. You said yourself, Jack, these psychos are very clever. Billy's probably made bombs before. I think it's real.'

Billy, waving his hands to the crowd: 'EVERYONE STAND BACK!'

Billy and Pete made their way to the area where Lenny Pazazz was interviewing Dutch Michael. They stopped in front of the two men wearing headphones, looking terrified. Their cordial interview had come to an abrupt ending and now they were faced with these two kimono wearing men who looked highly dangerous.

Billy: 'Remove your headphones.'

Lenny and Michael removed their headphones. They then attempted to get up from their chairs. 'Sit down!' Billy commanded. He then looked at Lenny Pazazz. 'You, go over there!' Lenny Pazazz, speechless and terrified, got up and disappeared into the crowd. And then Billy did something that drew screams from the Thai girls. He pulled out his machete from a holster inside his robe, pointed it at the terrified Dutchman and said, 'You….stay!'

Within moments, Pete had placed the bomb on the table, and

pulled out a pair of handcuffs. He roughly cuffed Michael's hands behind his back. 'What are you doing? What is this about?' Michael whimpered. Billy put the blade of the machete next to Michael's face and made a silence gesture.

Billy, to the terrified Dutchman: 'You, stand up!' Michael did as he was told. 'Turn around and face the crowd. Walk three paces and get on your knees.'

The crowd in the bar were shocked at what they were seeing. No one had any idea what this was all about. All they knew was that these were a couple of wackos, but dangerous wackos, with knives and a bomb. And this was a frightening situation they were now in.

Billy observed the camera man, a young Thai. This was the guy who was beaming this show out to thousands of people across the world. This show was then going to be recorded and probably shared by millions. This was the video man who was going to make Billy famous.

Billy, to the cameraman: 'You! Point the camera this way!' The young Thai cameraman pointed his expensive video camera towards Billy and the kneeling Dutchman. 'Keep filming. I want the world to see this.'

There was silence for a moment. The crowd of farangs and Thai girls stood and watched. Billy stood tall, menacing, with the machete waving in his hand. Pete stood solid, holding the bomb in one hand and a long knife in the other. He had been taught well by his mentor. He now looked threatening. Billy looked around at everyone. It was all in place. The crowd, the cameraman, the kneeling Dutchman, even Liberace looking shocked, sitting at his piano. He would be put to use, also. Now it was time for Billy to make his speech.

Billy, staring into the camera: 'People of the world, of Youtube, of Social Media, please share this video with everyone you know. I am Billy. And I want you to remember my face. Mine is the face of a man who believes in real justice, the kind of justice that is sadly lacking in today's pathetic world. And today I'm going to serve justice on a truly evil man. Keep watching this, and you will see the kind of justice that this world so badly needs.'

Billy held up his machete to the camera. He hoped that the image of his face holding the machete would become an iconic one. World famous. Legendary.

Billy, pulling a sheet of paper from his pocket and pointing to the kneeling Dutchman: 'You, Micheal Van Langren, from the Netherlands, are charged with committing the most heinous offences against women and minors.' This drew raised eyebrows and shocked faces from the crowd. 'You are guilty of not only possessing child pornography, but indeed creating it. For this crime you served a paltry sentence in a Dutch prison.' Billy looked up at the shocked faces. 'I think, ladies and gentlemen, that alone is enough to make our blood boil. This man served minimum time for perpetrating the suffering of children. A travesty of a sentence, I think you will all agree.' He then turned back to his paper. 'You, Michael Van Langren, have been accused of the trafficking of women, children and others. My own friend here, Peter, has himself been a victim of your human slavery, perpetrated for the gratification of wealthy perverts in one of your sordid Sado Masochistic clubs.'

Again the crowd looked shocked, shuffling about uneasily. And then Pete did something which wasn't in the script. He stepped forward, still holding the bomb, and kicked Michael in the back of the head. Micheal yelped and fell forward. Billy turned to Pete: 'Easy, my friend.' He then turned to the crowd. 'As you can see, my friend is emotional even at the very mention of the ordeal he suffered at the hands of this evil man.'

Billy put the sheet of paper away. He held his machete up for the camera once more. He'd made his point. He had the crowd on his side by now. It was now time for a bit more theatrics. Billy turned to Liberace, sitting at the piano, wondering how his show could have ended up like this. 'You, Mr Piano man, I want you to play, 'Shall we gather at the river.' Liberace couldn't speak. It took him a few seconds to realise the scary man was talking to him. 'Do you know, 'Shall we gather at the river'?' Liberace eventually nodded, his face white with shock. 'Then play it.'

And then the music began. Liberace, the terrified tribute performer, began banging away at his piano and the bar was suddenly filled with music. 'Sing it!' Billy commanded. 'Everyone, sing. Shall we gather at the river.'

And Liberace, the crowd, everyone, joined in the hym: 'Shall we gather at the river.'

At the other side of the bar there were mixed emotions of shock, horror, fear and total disbelief. Seamus, the grumpy sidekick of Lenny Pazazz, whispered to the bar owner: 'Lenny, I'm looking at the viewing figures on my mobile. Word of mouth must be spreading. The viewing figures are going through the roof.'

Lenny, whimpering: 'Oh, My God. I knew something like this would happen sooner or later. We have to be careful about our guests. We should never have invited that pervert to come here.'

Seamus: 'Oh, stop whinging. This will get you another hundred thousand subscribers. Then you can start paying me some of that long awaited money you owe me.'

'Shall we gather at the riiiiiiver.'
Billy: 'COME ON, SING! SING, YOU FUCKERS!'

Jack, shaking his head: 'Fucking hell, I knew this guy was wacko, but I never expected this.'

Kenny: 'Like you said, Jack, these psychos are very clever. He's planned all this to the last detail.'

Joey, singing: 'Shall we gather at the river... I know this song, good choice.'

Vinnie: 'What? You know this song?'

Joey, looking uncharacteristically pensive: 'Yes. I mean, the old couple at the farm...they taught it to me. We sang it at the piano together.'

Vinnie, rolling his eyes: 'Oh, so that's where the Bible comes into it. For fuck's sake, I never thought my friend Joey would become a praying Jesus.'

Joey, moving with the song: 'Well, you gotta believe in something.'

Kenny: 'For fuck's sake Joey, this is not the time to be joining in with the song.'

Carol: 'What the fuck is going on here?'

Lizzy: 'I knew it. We've been led into a fucking trap!'

Carol: 'What? How's it a trap?'

Lizzy, stoned faced angry: 'Don't you see? You've been shagging these Scousers and now we're here being held hostage by two more Scousers. Don't you see the connection?'

Carol: 'No. And I've only been shagging two Scousers, not the whole lot of them.'

Lizzy: 'Well I reckon there's more to it than they're letting on. All as bad as each other. Fucking Scousers.'

Vinnie: 'I reckon it's not a real bomb. I say we all rush the door, remove all those tables out the way and get the fuck out of here.'

Jack: 'I thought you said it's not a real bomb.'

Vinnie: 'Well, erm, erm....' Vinnie run out of ideas as quick as they came.

'SHALL WE GATHER AT THE RIVER...WHERE BRIGHT ANGEL FEET HAVE TROD' Billy was loving it. The piano man was getting a real rhythm going. Even the crowd appeared to love it. This was going well, Billy thought. 'Come on, sing, everyone sing.'

'WITH IT'S CRYSTAL TIDE FOREVER....FLOWING BY THE THRONE OF GOD.'

The crowd were really getting into the song. This bar was full of mostly bald headed, middle aged farangs who came here to meet Lenny Pazazz, the camp guy who they'd seen on Youtube, and maybe barfine one of the bar's hotties in the process. Who would have thought they would be here tonight, singing some decrepit old hymn and waiting for a nonce to have his head chopped off live on air? Truth is, Billy had thought long and hard about the theatrical side of it all. He had chosen 'Shall We Gather At The River' after hearing it sung in the shockingly violent opening scene in one of his favourite movies, The Wild Bunch. It seemed to add to the drama.

Lenny Pazazz, whimpering: 'This is bad! This is very bad, Seamus! We are being set up for something very bad to happen.'

Seamus, groaning: 'Well, one of them's holding a bomb, so I suppose that's bad enough.'

Lenny: 'Oh, Seamus, you're making light of all this. This is my bar, my Youtube channel, my everything. This will destroy everything I have.'

Seamus: 'Aww, relax. One of the girls has just phoned the police. They're on their way here. Now look at the viewing figures. Wow, we're up to almost ten thousand viewers! Wow, Youtube is really pushing the stream out there. Soon everyone will be watching.'

Lenny: 'Ten thousand viewers. Wow, that's amazing.'

Seamus: 'Thought that would cheer you up, you money grabbing wuss.'

PATTAYA POLICE STATION

At Pattaya City Police station, Captain Pongsapat Tanasugarn was sitting at his desk, eating a pot of 7/11 noodles and watching a rerun of Manchester United v Bournemouth on the TV when he got the call. Disturbance at Lenny's bar, Soi 13. British men holding hostages. One has a machete and the other a bomb.

Captain Tanasugarn quickly ate more of his spicy noodles before cursing and throwing the pot in the bin. He got up abruptly from his chair. 'Fucking farangs,' he growled.

Minutes later half a dozen police vehicles tore through the streets of Pattaya, sirens screaming, headed for Soi 13.

The song finished. Billy smiled. 'A big round of applause for our wonderful pianist Liberace, everybody.' The crowd all broke into spontaneous applause. This wasn't so bad after all, some people thought. So one of these nutters had a bomb, so what?

Billy, waving his machete about: 'Okay everyone, thank you all.

That was wonderful singing. And now we have more musical accompaniment. I would like to ask our pianist here to start playing the famous Funeral March, composed by Beethoven.' Billy looked at Liberace. 'Play it.'

Everyone in the crown looked at each other, as if things were about to get really, really dramatic. A small, pudgy man stepped forward from the crowd and said, 'Actually, it wasn't Beethoven who composed the Funeral March. It was Chopin.' Billy gave him an evil stare, and the man quickly hurried back to his chair.

'Play it,' Billy said again. Liberace looked terrified as he began playing the Funeral March, dreading where this was all going.

Billy looked down on the pathetic, sobbing, kneeling figure of Dutch Michael. 'You: do you know the words to the Lord's Prayer?'

Dutch Micheal shook his head and sobbed. 'No….no, Sir…'

Billy: 'Thought not.' He nodded to Pete, who pulled out a sheet of paper and held it in front of Michael. 'Now, read it. It begins with Our Father, who art in Heaven.'

The crowd were motionless. If anyone thought this was a joke then no one was laughing now. The Funeral March was playing, a sobbing man was kneeling with his hands cuffed behind his back, and now he was being forced to recite the Lords Prayer.

Dutch Michael: 'Our Father….sob…who….Are….Heaven.. I can't…can't read this…'

Billy, raising the machete in a dramatic sudden movement which drew gasps from the crowd: 'SAY IT! HALLOWED BE THY NAME! SAY IT!'

The Dutchman sobbed uncontrollably and through slobber he attempted to read the sheet of paper Pete dangled in front of him.

And the Funeral March played solemnly while the crowd stood motionless, silent, watching.

Kenny: 'We got to do something. Jack, we got to do something. This is crazy.'

Jack: 'You tell me. What are we gonna do? Do you have any

ideas?'

Joey: 'It was your idea to bring us here, Jack. Now go talk to Billy and tell him to stop.'

Jack, alarmed at the suggestion: 'What? You're having a laugh, aren't you? Billy doesn't trust me, I'm the one he trusts least out of all of us. He'll probably behead me for being a traitor or something.'

Vinnie: 'I can hear sirens. The bizzies are on the way.'

Jack: 'That's the answer, I'm afraid. The police are coming. Let them sort it out.'

Lizzy, more angry by the minute: 'This is fucking stupid! Carol, I'm never coming on holiday with you ever again. This is a fucking disaster!'

Carol, aware of Lizzy's temper when she was angry: 'Don't blame me, Lizzy. I didn't want to come to this shithole, either.'

Lizzy: 'But you've made it worse. If it wasn't bad already, you're shagging these two twats, my husband is shagging prostitutes behind my back and now were trapped here with this fucking mental case and his mate threatening to blow us all up. For fuck's sake, I'm fucking getting out of here.'

Carol: 'Lizzy, cool down. Just stay where you are. You can't get out or they might let that bomb off.'

Joey: 'Yes, stay cool, Lizzy. You can't start moving all those tables from the doorway or these nutters will blow us all up.'

Lizzy, angrily to Joey: 'Who the fuck do think your talking to? Don't talk down to me, you fucking Scouse prick. You couldn't even get a hard on without spewing your guts out.'

That was an episode Joey didn't want to remember, but he decided not to agitate Lizzy anymore. She was probably more explosive than the bomb.

There was a loud bang on the door of the bar. The police had arrived. Liberace stopped playing, making Billy angry. 'Don't stop playing!' he growled. Liberace resumed the Funeral March, while the sobbing Dutchman continued his attempt at the Lord's Prayer.

Billy stared solemnly into the camera. 'So, you see, people of the world, I want you to record this livestream and share it with whoever you can. I want the world to see this moment, this pivotal moment in time, this landmark of justice. I want everyone across the world to see the justice, the perfect justice, served upon this evil man called Michael Van Langren. And I want you to remember my face, and that of my friend. We are Billy and Peter, two ordinary lads from Liverpool. We have had our woes and our problems, but together, we realise that we must make a stand. And we must deliver the kind of justice the evil people of this world so deserve. And we are beginning with this evil man, Michael Van Langen.'

Michael completed The Lord's Prayer. Pete stepped back. Billy raised the machete suddenly in the air. The crowd gasped. Liberace stumbled on his piano keys. The police continued banging on the door.

Lenny Pazazz, clasping his hand to his mouth: 'Oh, Seamus, I think I'm going to be sick. I can't watch.'

Seamus: 'Aww, grow a pair, we're in the middle of something famous. You'll be boasting about it next week.'

Kenny: 'Jesus, he's gonna cut his head off. What are we gonna do….?'

No one, not Jack, Joey, Vinnie or Carol had an answer. But Lizzy had other ideas.

Lizzy, irascible and hot tempered: 'For fuck's sake, I've had enough of this! I'm getting out of this fucking shithole now!'

Carol, always worried about her best friend: 'Lizzy, just cool down, the police are coming, it'll all be over soon.'

Lizzy: 'Fuck the police and fuck all these stupid fucking Scousers!'

Everyone looked around at Lizzy in alarm. You sure wouldn't want to get on the wrong side of this woman when she was angry. But then Lizzy did something that no man in that bar had the balls to do. She slammed her beer bottle down on the table, pushed and shoved her huge bulk through the crowd and whoever was in her way, and marched angrily over to Billy, the madman with the machete in his hand.

Lizzy, red faced and furious: 'HEY, YOU! FUCK FACE! WHAT THE FUCK DO YOU THINK YOU'RE PLAYING AT, YOU FUCKING SCOUSE PRICK?'

Everything went silent. The piano playing came to an abrupt halt. The crowd stood still, speechless. Liberace's mouth fell open, Pete stood motionless with the bomb in his hand. And Billy, holding the machete high above his head, suddenly found himself gazing at something he hadn't counted for. And then, slowly, his perplexed expression cracked into a smile, and he began laughing heartily.

Lizzy, fuming: 'DON'T START LAUGHING! NOW OPEN THOSE FUCKING DOORS AND LET US ALL OUT OF HERE. I'VE FUCKING HAD ENOUGH OF THIS SHIT!'

Billy, grinning: 'And who might you be, fine lady?'

Lizzy: 'WHAT? DON'T TAKE THE FUCKING PISS, EITHER!'

Billy was amused. This intrusion he hadn't counted for, but no great event would be complete without its comic incidents. He grinned and looked around at the crowd. 'Well, well, what a remarkable intrusion this is,' Billy said, lowering the machete. 'And who would have thought this, eh? Amongst all you big, brave men, it has taken a woman to stand up and be counted.' Billy laughed. 'What a fine example of female bravery this is. This lady here is remarkable, and I want you all to remember her tremendous courage in the face of adversary.' Billy grinned at the red, ugly, angry face of Lizzy. 'And what, may I ask, is your name, fine lady?'

Lizzy: 'FUCK THE NAME! NOW OPEN THAT FUCKING DOOR!'

Billy, unfazed: 'No, no, lady. You must tell us all your name. We are here at an monumental event that will forever be recorded and go down in history. Now, at least tell me your name, please.'

Lizzy: 'IT'S LIZZY, OKAY? HAPPY NOW? THE NAME'S LIZZY.'

Billy, grinning and nodding: 'Lizzy. So your name is Lizzy. Thank you.' He then turned to the crowd and said, 'Everyone here, I'd like you all to give a big round of applause for BIG LIZZY.

Come on, everybody, let's hear it. Put your hands together for BIG LIZZY'

The crowd broke out into spontaneous applause.

At the back of the bar, mouths fell open. Carol looked at Joey, a shocked expression on her face. Vinnie looked at Carol, Joey looked at Jack, Jack looked at Kenny.

Carol: 'He's just called her Big Lizzy.'

Vinnie, nodding: 'Yes, he did call her Big Lizzy.'

Joey, wincing: 'He did definitely call her Big Lizzy.'

And that was the straw that broke the camel's back. In one heated moment all the rage Lizzy felt at her truly shit holiday, her husband shagging Thai prostitutes, fucking Scousers, being mistaken for a lesbian, everything that made her angry, and now that final insult to be called the name that had haunted her since childhood, came out and exploded with one mighty left hook which slammed into Billy's jaw and sent him flying backwards over a table.

Billy, the psychopath who had planned to cut off the head of a sex offender live on air and make himself a hero, was now lying unconscious, flat on his back on the floor, his beloved machete by his side. He had been knocked out by a woman.

The crowd suddenly became animated, people were getting up from their chairs and moving about.

Pete, holding up the bomb: 'WAIT! DON'T ANYBODY MOVE! I HAVE THE BOMB!'

There were gasps from the crowd. No one knew what would happen next. And then Jack walked out of the crowd and marched straight up to Pete. He stopped and stared at Pete, an angry look on Jack's face. Jack grabbed the bomb in Pete's hand, wrestled with him for it, and then Jack held the bomb up to the crowd. Everyone gasped. A few of the Thai girls were screaming and crying.

Pete, a pathetic look on his frightened face: 'Jack. We are mates, aren't we, Jack?'

Jack hit Pete across the jaw with the bomb with a loud crack that sent Pete to the floor. 'Not any more,' Jack said.

With both of the clowns lying unconscious on the floor and the Thai police banging the door down, Jack turned to face the crowd. He pulled off the cloth bag covering the bomb and held up the bomb to the crowd. It was a tin of peaches. He then pulled off the ring tab and opened the tin. He put his fingers inside and produced a peach slice and began eating it. He then ate another, looked at the shocked crowd and said, 'Yummy.'

It was pandemonium at Lenny's bar for the rest of the evening. It seemed the whole world and his dog had turned up, wanting to know what had happened.

The Thai police arrested Billy and Pete and bundled them away to the cells. The machete, knives and the open tin of peaches were also seized as evidence.

There were TV reporters present, news crews, people being interviewed. The bar had swollen with customers from other bars wanting to share in a bit of excitement.

The lads decided to hang on and order another round of drinks. Jack was approached by a glamorous Thai lady with a microphone in her hand and a camera crew behind her.

Thai woman: 'Hello. I hear you are the man who dismantled the bomb.'

Jack, who'd had a few beers by now, looked at this well dressed, smiling, good looking Thai woman. He didn't know what to say. So he laughed out loud. It was all he could think of to do. And that's where Joey stepped in. Grinning, chuckling, wanting to be on camera to show everyone how handsome he is.

Joey: 'Hi, my name's Joey.'

Thai woman: 'Hi. Who are you?'

Joey, eyeing up the Thai beauty in front of him: 'I was here. I saw it all.'

Thai woman: 'Yes. We have heard what happened. So what was your part in all of this?'

Joey, looking into this Thai beauties eyes, hoping for a bit of sexual connection: 'Well, I'll give you an interview if you want. So long as the interview is with you. You seem like a very professional lady' He put on his best, most photogenic smile for the camera and gave a little wave. You never know, a top modelling agency could be watching. Could lead to something big.

The glamorous Thai woman eventually got tired of Joey, and turned her microphone to other customers.

'Bastard,' Joey said under his breath.

Lenny Pazazz and his grumpy sidekick Seamus were being interviewed by one of the top TV networks in Thailand. The TV man spoke to Lenny. 'So you are the owner of this bar and were doing a live Youtube show. You must have been terrified when these vicious men all of a sudden appeared in your bar.'

Lenny, standing tall and dignified: 'Well, I must admit, it was a bit unnerving at first, but as a bar owner you are dealing with the public constantly and when something like this happens you have to show your strength of character. You need to remain calm in a situation like this.'

Seamus, cringing at Lenny; 'Strength of character? Remaining calm? You were under the table and whimpering like a big girl's blouse, for fuck's sake.'

Lenny smiled for the camera, embarrassed.

CHAPTER TWELVE

WE ARE ALL GONNA MISS THIS PLACE

Ning was angry. She was really angry.

Lee had grown wise to her and stopped sending her money. He had sent text messages to tell her it was over and he didn't want anything to do with her again. That meant a loss of money for her. Okay, she had other sponsors and could easily work on getting more. But Lee was a loss, a big loss because she was about to push him for more money.

And then there was Tomas, the German blackmailer. He was still threatening to send nude pictures of Ning to her family if she didn't pay back all the sponsor money he sent her. This was a real problem. But nothing that a wily girl like Ning couldn't sort out.

So Ning arranged to meet Tomas in a quiet bar in Soi 13. They could talk things over. It was a bar Ning knew well. It was the same bar in which Jack and Kenny had a row with the Thai barman and his hoods. A bar which had a less than savoury reputation.

So Ning took a seat at the bar, the only customer there on a quiet evening. And it wasn't long before Tomas turned up, grinning as he walked through the door.

'Is that him?' the Thai barman whispered to Ning.

Ning, grinning maliciously: 'Yes, that's him.'

As Tomas took a seat next to Ning at the bar, the Thai barman got on his mobile phone. Two minutes later two of his Thai hoods entered the bar. The barman locked the door after them and pulled the shutter down.

Tomas, observing the rough looking Thai men: 'What's happening? Why are you closing the bar?'

Truth is these three hoods were associates of Ning. And Tomas had done something it is most unwise to do in Thailand. He had got on the wrong side of Thai people.

THE NEXT DAY

Jack, to Carol: 'Must admit, your mate Lizzy was the real hero in all of this. She deserves a medal for what she did. None of the guys had the guts to do it.'

Carol: 'She's a gentle giant when you get on the right side of her. That nutter just said the wrong thing at the wrong time!'

There were five of them sitting at a bar in Soi Six, Pattaya's red light strip lined with bars, girls, and short time rooms upstairs. They were in good spirits. The lads holiday was coming to an end and it seemed the problems had been ironed out. They hadn't heard any more of the big fight they were involved in and the Yorkshireman who was on a life support machine. The lads guessed that, if he recovered, he would be too embarrassed to admit he lost a fight. And, besides, the guy who had battered him was now in police custody. No one, neither Jack, Kenny, Joey or Vinnie seemed worried about it anymore. Just enjoy the rest of the time here.

Joey: 'I've decided to stay here. I'm not going back home.'

They all looked at Joey, thinking the same thoughts. What about visas? What about money? What about work? Had Joey really considered any of these things?

Vinnie: 'I'm staying here, as well. I'm getting shit from from my ex wife back home.' Vinnie didn't tell the lads it is because he stole his ex wife's jewellery and the police were now after him. 'I don't see I've got anything to lose. I'm staying in Thailand. There's got to be something going on here I can do.'

Jack: 'Like what?'

Vinnie: 'Like teach English. I've heard of guys doing that.'

Jack drank his beer and said nothing. When he thought of it, Vinnie could talk his way into anything, he had that personality. Jack wouldn't be surprised if he got a job teaching English. Only Vinnie's change of plan mentality and wacky baccy addiction would let him down. As for Joey, they all knew he was on the run from Liverpool gangsters. Owed a lot of money to the wrong people. He was probably safer here ducking and diving.

Kenny: 'I've got to go home. But I'll be back here. Won't be long. Say what you want about Pattaya, it's a damn good crack.'

Jack: 'I agree. I'll keep coming back here again and again.' He chuckled. 'There's never a dull moment.'

Carol: 'Well, I'm coming out here to live once I divorce that waste of space I'm with.' She touched the legs of Joey and Vinnie. 'I've got two reasons to come back here,' she grinned.

They all laughed. This woman had no shame, but so what? She knew what she liked. What's so bad about that?

Kenny, to Carol: 'So where's your mate, then? I thought you'd be with her today. We all wanted to buy her a drink for being such a hero.'

Carol, shrugging: 'Not sure. Last I heard of her she was looking for George. He keeps swanning off. She's got this idea he's shagging Thai girls behind her back.'

Three bars away from where the group were sitting, there was a massive commotion in one of the Soi 6 bars. It involved a big, angry English woman storming in, shouting and swearing and frightening all the girls and bars staff. The angry woman stormed upstairs, kicked in various doors to rooms where farangs and Thai girls were going about their sexual business until she finally found what she was looking for. In one of the upstairs short time rooms, there was her husband, George. The sight of his naked, weedy little body pounding away at a Thai prostitute sent Lizzy in a rage that shook the building. There were screams and yells and shouting and George being dragged off the unfortunate Thai girl and shoved down the stairs. The bar staff went into a panic when they witnessed this terrifying, hysterical monster of a woman whacking a puny, naked little man across the bar and out into the street.

Carol and the lads were in good spirits, enjoying their drinks when they heard the commotion. It began with the loud, hysterical bellows of Lizzy, and then they saw George, naked as the day he was born, being shoved and slapped around Soi 6. It was quite a spectacle, stopping the traffic in the narrow street, as this puny naked little man was being viciously assaulted by this ferocious big woman.

Joey, laughing: 'Oh, fucking hell, I've seen everything now!'

Kenny, laughing: 'So that's where she's been. Doing the Private Detective on her husband.'

Carol, laughing as Lizzy kicked George's naked arse up the street: 'Oh, my God. I always thought George had a little willy but I didn't know it was that little.'

It was a hilarious spectacle, and drew the attention from everyone in Soi 6. Farangs in the bars stood up to see the show, laughing and jeering. Thai girls came out of the bars to have a good laugh. The only two people who weren't laughing were George, who was getting a battering from his wife, and Lizzy, whose anger and humiliation had reached boiling point.

Lizzy, whacking George up the street: 'BASTARD! DIRTY LITTLE BASTARD!' She then turned her anger to the laughing farangs and Thai girls in the bars. 'SLAGS! SLAGS! FUCKING SLAGS!

Jack, Kenny, Joey, Vinnie, Carol and everyone who witnessed this spectacle was laughing hysterically. They'd had a good holiday but this was the icing on the cake.

Jack: 'I can't wait to come back here again.'

Kenny: 'Never a dull moment in Pattaya.'

And Lizzy continued to teach her naked little husband a lesson he would never forget. Whack: 'SLAGS!' Whack! 'SLAGS!' Whack! 'FUCKING SLAGS! SLAGS! SLAGS! SLAGS!'

EPILOGUE

Basket Case Billy and his sidekick Pete hit the world headlines. It wasn't such a dreadful crime, more of an oddball story of a psycho trying to get famous by threatening to decapitate a sex offender live on air whilst his mate threatened everyone with a bomb that turned out to be a tin of peaches! Whatever it was all about, it got Billy and Pete inevitably banged up and facing a very long stretch in a most unpleasant Thai prison.

Dutch Michael, the intended victim, suffered a terrifying ordeal which left him a nervous wreck. But that wasn't all he had to suffer. His ladyboy bar couldn't open because of a police investigation into his alleged shady activities. The bad publicity didn't help, either.

As for Lenny Pazazz, he came out smiling. The invasion in his bar and the world headlines had boosted his beloved Youtube Channel and doubled his subscribers overnight. This brought him more ad revenue, more customers, more fame, more everything. The only downside was that Seamus, a shareholder in Lenny's company, now wanted more money for organising his shows. Ah, well, every silver lining has its cloud.

Vinnie decided to take a chance and began hitchhiking around Thailand, bumming money from fellow farangs and getting some casual teaching work. He was on a wing and a prayer and wasn't concerned about the fact he had overstayed his Thai visa. But he was determined to make something of himself in Thailand, simply because he had nothing else. He couldn't afford the flight back to England and would be facing the police for having stolen his wife's jewellery. His motto was, just take every day as it comes.

As for Joey, he couldn't go back to the UK, either, for fear of being done in by loan sharks. But he'd grown to like Thailand and, like Vinnie, didn't let minor issues like visas and stuff prevent him from staying here. And he had found a new career out here. Carol wasn't a one off, there were more than a few middle aged western women who felt out of place and would love nothing more than to encounter a handsome young Englishman to satisfy their needs. So Joey decided he was going to carve out a new career as a gigolo, right here in Pattaya. How could he fail?

Kenny and Jack, more level headed than the other clowns, went back to the UK thinking that had been another great holiday and it wouldn't be long before they'd be planning the next one. They decided to keep in touch with Lee, their new mate, who, although he'd had his heart broken, had wised up and found himself forty thousand baht better off each month.

Tomas, the German blackmailer, was also given a lesson he wouldn't forget. A lesson that led to him being hospitalised with broken bones courtesy of Ning's thuggish friends. In fact, what made matters worse is that he didn't have any insurance, and was desperately trying to convince his parents to remortgage their house so he could be treated and flown home.

And Ning carried on doing what she did best. She had lost some sponsors, but what the hell? There's plenty more mugs where those mugs came from.

As for Carol and Jeff, they continued together, in spite of all the hostility. Similar with Lizzy and George. When the dust settles, even the strangest relationships concede it's better the devil you know.

As for Jack, he was faced with a huge decision. What should he do about Minnie? He knew the script for sending money to Thai girls was a mug's game. Look at poor Lee. But Jack still felt he had to look after her. He couldn't bear the thought of her walking the streets looking for business. So he did the thing he said he would never do. He agreed to send her money each month. Fifty thousand baht, more than a grand a month in

English money. Enough for Minnie to live on in rural Thailand.

Minnie: 'Jack, I love you. I want to go England with you.'

Jack, looking into Minnie's beautiful face: 'I've got a better idea. I'm coming to live in Thailand with you.'

Minnie, surprised: 'What? You come live here in Thailand?'

Jack: 'Soon, Minnie. I've had enough of England like so many others have. So when I get back I'm going to sell everything and come out here to live. With you.'

Minnie's face lit up: 'Jack. That's wonderful?'

Minnie hugged Jack, and Jack knew at the moment that this girl was not like Ning. Because not all Thai girls are the same, just as not all English girls are the same. Minnie was genuine, and Jack genuinely believed that. And, as he hugged his girlfriend, the girl he wanted to settle with in this wonderful country of Thailand, he resolved that he himself would change. He would learn to trust people. Not all, just a few. And Minnie was one of those few. And the next time he came to Thailand he'd be here to stay. With the love of his life, Minnie.

AND FINALLY: BRING ME THE HEAD OF LAUGHING BOY

A BIG POSH HOUSE IN WOOLTON, LIVERPOOL

Liverpool has some fine, posh areas. One of them is Woolton, a leafy suburb with some very imposing houses. You need big money to live here.

In one of the most impressive big houses, with gates and a huge, perfectly maintained garden, the owner of the house used it not just as his home, but as the headquarters of his lucrative, and often shady real estate business.

Freddy Gibson rocked his huge bulk in his chair as he observed his laptop on his desk whilst fondling a busty young blonde. It was good being a rich gangster. Money, cars, birds, and the ability to put fear, or even wipe out, those who crossed you. Freddy Gibson, head of the Gibson brothers' shady property empire, has done them all, first hand.

There was a knock at the door. Freddy grunted. In walked one of his henchmen, looking like he had urgent news for his boss.

Henchman: 'Boss, have you seen the news? About that incident in Thailand. That Pattaya place.'

Freddy, squeezing the young blonde's titties: 'I heard something. Couple of Scousers acting the goat in a foreign country. So what's new?'

Henchman, excited: 'Did you watch the news report on it? The bit where the Thai woman reporter interviewed people in the bar?'

Freddy, looking uninterested: 'Not exactly. Anything I really need to watch it for?'

Henchman: 'Just have a look at the news clip on Youtube. I think you WILL find it interesting.'

Freddy yawned and would have told his sidekick to take a hike. But he got Youtube up on his laptop. 'Now what?'

Henchman, scrolling down the screen: 'This one.' He clicked on it and enlarged the video so his boss could watch it.

Freddy Gibson watched the Youtube video news clip on his laptop whilst sitting at his desk and fondling a young blonde. And he watched the glamorous female Thai reporter interviewing people in the aftermath of a bomb scare at a bar in a country he had never visited. And he watched closely, and pretty soon he was interested. And as Freddy glared at the screen he began clenching his teeth, and his grip tightened on his pen and he began slowly, angrily banging his fist on his desk.

Henchman, noticing his boss's anger: 'It's him, isn't it, boss? It's that fucking prick who done a runner with your money.'

Freddy Gibson glared at the laptop screen. He saw the Thai reporter, the farangs in the bar, and there, speaking to the reporter, laughing, sneering, waving at the camera, vying for attention, was Joey, the weasel who had cheated him out of thousands of pounds. Tens of thousands of pounds. No shame, no shyness for the camera, no concern about who might see him, this cheeky piece of shit was there in Thailand, putting two fingers up to whoever.

Freddy, seething: 'How much money does this piece of shit owe us by now?'

Henchman: 'Last time I looked, the interest had rocketed out of control. It must be edging towards a hundred grand by now.'

Freddy sat back, fuming. He broke away from his young blonde and switched the video off. He looked around his plush office for a moment, clenched his mighty fists and then said: 'I don't care about the money. I want that Laughing Boy dead. I want him dead, strangled, drowned, I don't care what. I'm going to make an example of him. That piece of shit has humiliated me. And I'm not gonna let that go. So he's living it up in Thailand, then, is he? Well, that's good. Because that will prove our influence even more. It will prove that, no matter where you are in the world, you can run but you can't hide. You can't hide from the Gibby's. You cross us, we'll find you and wipe you off the face of the fucking Earth.'

Henchman: 'So what are you gonna do, boss?'

Freddy Gibson sat back in his chair: 'Who do we know in this place in Thailand?'

Henchman: 'There's Tommy Grimes. He owns a nightclub, amongst other things, in Bangkok. That's only a couple of hours drive away from Pattaya.'

Freddy thought for a moment: 'Tommy Grimes. He's been out there a while, hasn't he? Good old lad, Tommy. He owes me a few favours.'

Henchman: 'I'll get in touch with him for you. Tommy knows all that's going on out there. He'll sort out that piece of shit for you. Hit men are ten a penny out there, boss. It shouldn't be a problem.'

Freddy, nodding thoughtfully: 'That's good. That's good. Get in touch with Tommy ASAP. Tell him to put his best man on the job. I'll pay handsomely.' Freddy banged his fist on the desk. 'I want Laughing Boy's head on a plate: TONIGHT!'

THE END